© Morgan Roberts

Dr Anita Heiss is an internationally published, award-winning author/editor of over 20 books: non-fiction, historical fiction, commercial women's fiction and children's novels. She is a proud member of the Wiradyuri Nation of central New South Wales, an Ambassador for the Indigenous Literacy Foundation and the GO Foundation, and Professor of Communications at the University of Queensland. Anita is also the Publisher at Large of Bundyi, an imprint of Simon & Schuster cultivating First Nations talent. As an artist in residence at La Boite Theatre, she adapted her novel *Tiddas* for the stage. It premiered at the 2022 Brisbane Festival and was produced by Belvoir St Theatre for the Sydney Festival in 2024. Her novel, *Bila Yarrudhanggalangdhuray*, about the Great Flood of Gundagai, won the 2022 NSW Premier's Indigenous Writer's Prize and was shortlisted for the 2021 ARA Historical Novel Prize and the 2022 ABIA Awards. Anita's first children's picture book is *Bidhi Galing* (*Big Rain*), also about the Great Flood of Gundagai. Anita's historical novel *Dirrayawadha* (*Rise Up*) was released in 2024. Anita enjoys running, eating chocolate and being a creative disruptor.

# Red Dust Running

## Anita Heiss

**SIMON & SCHUSTER**

New York · Amsterdam/Antwerp · London · Toronto · Sydney · New Delhi

RED DUST RUNNING
First published in Australia in 2023 by Audible Australia Proprietary Limited
This edition published in 2025 by Simon & Schuster (Australia) Pty Limited
Level 4, 32 York St, Sydney NSW 2000

10 9 8 7 6 5 4 3 2 1

New York Amsterdam/Antwerp London Toronto Sydney New Delhi
Visit our website at www.simonandschuster.com.au

© Anita Heiss 2023

All rights reserved. No part of this publication may be reproduced, stored in a retrieval system, or transmitted in any form or by any means, electronic, mechanical, photocopying, recording or otherwise, without prior permission of the publisher.

 A catalogue record for this book is available from the National Library of Australia

ISBN: 9781761631382

Cover design: Christa Moffitt, Christabella Designs
Cover images: Woman, Shutterstock/Bibadash; Hat, Shutterstock/Bibadash; Feather, Shutterstock/Gst01
Typeset by Midland Typesetters, Australia
Printed and bound in Australia by Griffin Press

 The paper this book is printed on is certified against the Forest Stewardship Council® Standards. Griffin Press holds chain of custody certification SCS-COC-001185. FSC® promotes environmentally responsible, socially beneficial and economically viable management of the world's forests.

# CHAPTER ONE

'You can't keep running away, Annabelle!' Angel's hands are on her hips, but her tone is gentle, as always. She's my favourite cousin and the only person who gets away with giving me a good talking-to.

'Why not?' I ask. It's not the first time I've heard this lecture and it probably won't be the last. I'm unwrapping coffee mugs on autopilot and rinsing them in the sink as we talk.

'Because you're 35 and need to settle down, be a grown-up, and *try* to sort issues out occasionally, instead of running away and leaving unresolved shit behind.' Angel rarely swears, so I know she's serious.

I finally turn to face her, hoping our reunion after all these years doesn't end in an argument. Neither of us like conflict.

'What do you want me to do? Settle down like you and Kev, with chickens and compost and crocs on my feet?'

I point to Angel's less-than-glamorous choice of footwear and smile. 'You know better than anyone, Angel, that's not my thing.' I dry the mugs as I consider the things I know about my cousin that we've agreed to keep in the vault over the years. 'And don't lecture me. You're no bloody angel, come to think of it.' I look at Angel's red lipstick, the only makeup she wears. Her smile is warm, her wavy charcoal hair rests on her shoulders, and her light blue cotton muumuu falls just below her knees. She looks much cooler than I feel in this heat.

'We're heeeere!'

Mandy James and Christine Jack, otherwise known as MJ and CJ, my two besties, my deadly tiddas, are standing on my newly rented doorstep. It's an old blonde-brick block of 12 units, with freshly painted stairs and railings, and I love seeing them through the screen door. CJ stands short with her tidy blonde bob. She's wearing a pink shoestring strap dress and holds a succulent. Next to her, MJ seems taller than ever in her jeans and tee, and her wild mass of sandy-coloured curls. She waves a bottle of bubbles in the air.

I immediately pull them into a tight, much-needed hug as soon as I swing the screen open. 'It's so good to see you, both,' I whisper, choked with the emotion of seeing them for the first time since returning to Magandjin. Four years living away without these women was just too long.

Within minutes, we are sitting on the floor, drinking the bubbly out of the coffee mugs. Unpacked boxes are scattered through the living room. Angel, a non-drinker, is sipping jasmine tea, thanks to the kettle she and Kev have given me as a house-warming gift.

'I knew you'd be back. Sydney is just too much for you,' MJ announces, then turns to CJ. 'I told you she'd rather be here, a big fish in a little pond. That's really why she likes Magandjin.'

CJ raises her mug in acknowledgment. Her noticeably toned arms prove that the early-morning workouts she complains about are paying off.

'It wasn't that,' Angel pipes up.

'What do you know that we don't?' MJ sounds like she's got her nose out of joint.

'I *am* her cousin, so there *will* be times that I know more, naturally.' Angel chuckles.

I turn to MJ and CJ. 'Before you ask – or worse, accuse! – I didn't do a runner in the middle of the night and leave a fella to wake up to find I was gone. So don't throw your judgement at me.'

They both look offended and shocked.

'And lose those gammon shocked looks,' I continue. 'I know you both too well. We've spent many, *many* sessions observing the good, the bad, *and* the ugly about each other and the world. Today is not one of those sessions.' I smile to let my inner circle know that it's all good.

'Go on then, tell us what happened,' they say in unison and laugh as if they'd scripted their double act.

'First of all, Nate, the guy in Sydney, was *different*.' I can hear how defensive I sound. 'I didn't want to break his heart, and *that's* why I left the way I did.'

Angel shakes her head. I know she thinks sneaking off in the middle of the night broke Nate's heart anyway.

My three tiddas stare at me in expectation, but I'm already tired of talking about my non-existent love life. 'I'm not going over old ground and old boyfriends with you lot. We've done those stories to death. And don't think I can't see your smirks behind every sip you take!' I say to CJ and MJ.

'What?' the two women jokingly protest.

'The thing is, I *had* to leave Sydney, and that job.' MJ cocks an eyebrow in question, and I sigh. There's no way to avoid this conversation. 'Fine. I'm only saying this once, so listen carefully.'

They all shuffle their butts along the newly cleaned carpet and huddle closer, like teenagers at a slumber party sharing ghost stories, or deep, dark secrets about first kisses.

I take a deep breath, then speak matter-of-factly. 'I had a relationship with one of the artists I was curating.' I exhale with the relief of the confession. 'When the mob found out, everyone assumed that he got the gig because he was sleeping with me, but the truth is we didn't even feel attracted to each other until opening night, literally a year after we signed contracts for the work. But the mob were brutal. They put pressure on the gallery and I was given an ultimatum, so I left. The job *and* the guy.' Angel opens her mouth but I cut her right off with a palm in her direction. 'I did *not* run away!'

I stand and extend a hand to help the others as they rise too. CJ looks at me empathetically, her dark brown eyes warm like her signature smile that makes her such a great schoolteacher. She winks, then turns to the others. 'How about she ran *towards* this fantastic new opportunity here in Magandjin?'

My face lights up at the mention of my new job. 'Thanks, CJ, that's the approach I'm taking. I can't wait to start at the gallery.' I begin unpacking a box of art books and stack them near where my bookcases will eventually be. 'And I have no doubt the Ancestors had this planned for me all along.'

My tiddas pitch in to help with the unpacking. Before long, I'm sweating up a storm. 'I can't stand this humidity,' I whine, setting off a string of complaints from the others.

'It's hideous!' 'Disgusting!' 'I'm melting!' they whinge.

A bead of sweat drips down the back of my leg. 'It's just this February heat that knocks me about. The humidity will be the end of me.'

The ever-practical MJ nods towards the air-conditioner and I dread the thought of the electricity bill. It's bad for the environment to be running it for hours every day.

'Let's just get some air,' I say, sliding the glass balcony doors wide open and waving them out. 'How cool is Paddington? It's exactly what I wanted in Sydney and could never afford. Only a few nights here and I already know 100 percent that this is where I want to be.' I breathe in the scent of freshly cut lawn. I love being in my semi-suburban street, yet so close to the city. I look at the poinsettia tree to the left and the jacaranda tree to the right, and I feel at home. 'I'm really happy to be here, really. And in some ways, you were right, MJ. Sydney was a bit too big for me, all those cars and people. I love that Magandjin is like a little country town, but with all the arts and culture we need. And all the tiddas I need, too.'

Angel puts her arm around my waist, and the four of us link together. Sistahood. I ran towards my beautiful friends, not away from anyone or anything. That's my story and I'm sticking to it.

'You're without a man, again,' MJ announces.

'Oh, for goodness' sake, I am the last person who needs a man to be happy,' I tell her. 'Nate was about sex, not happiness. My career, you tiddas, my life at large, that all makes me happy. If we did an audit of the men in my past, I think you'll find they've only ever caused me misery. This new journey, which I am *super* excited about, is about reaffirming my commitment to our mob in the arts, and rebuilding a little of my own self-esteem. Men are not even in my top five priorities right now.' I can see MJ looks suspicious, but I'm not giving this topic any more fuel. 'Let's talk about *your* love life, MJ?'

'Let's get back to unpacking your stuff instead,' she replies, always evasive about her own interludes of the romantic kind.

'Come on then, help me get the last of my things from my car. The removalists arrive tomorrow with the rest of my boxes and furniture.' We head back inside and towards the front door.

Angel starts humming a tune that none of us can name, but can easily join in. 'What's the song?' I ask.

'What's that tune about angels you're singing?' I ask Angel.

'Just something Kev sings to me as he makes my tea every morning.'

'Of course he does.' I push them out the door. MJ, CJ, and I all think Kev and Angel are perfectly matched. He's sensitive and strong, a guy who reads books and can build a bookcase as well.

We walk single file down the stairwell, one hand on the shoulder of the woman in front, and spill out onto the street, laughing and pushing each other out of the way like teenagers. You wouldn't know we were in our mid-30s. Angel has managed to get us all singing the chorus about morning angels as we lean into the back of my car, butts sticking out to passersby.

I pull out a heavy box of my favourite novels, the ones I refused to risk giving to the removalists, and lose my grip. My reflexes are quick as it slips, so it doesn't hit the ground. Then dark-skinned hands go over the top of mine and take the bulk of the weight.

'Nearly lost it,' a deep voice says, taking me by surprise. I lose my balance and my grip simultaneously.

The guy moves to steady me, but I swiftly pull away and let him take the full weight of the box as I step onto the footpath. 'Oh thanks, I think I can take it now.' I reach out, but he doesn't let the box go.

'Are you moving into number 5?' he asks.

'Yes, just settling in.'

He introduces himself as Michael from number 9, the unit above mine.

'I'm Annabelle, and this is MJ, CJ, and Angel.' I gesture to the others.

He's shifted the box to his hip and holds it with one hand, extending his other to shake theirs. MJ and CJ smirk. I roll my eyes, but I can't really blame them. I hope I'm being discreet as I take in Michael's fine form, his muscular arms and huge quads in his running shorts, his hazel eyes and tanned skin. I know he's a Murri without asking.

'I'll take this up on my way and leave it at the door,' he says to me. 'Anything you want to put on top of the box?'

I investigate the boot and pretend to search for something else. 'I think we're good, thanks!'

The four of us watch as Michael heads through the glass door with the books.

'Well, Michael is a good sort, eh?' MJ winks and licks her lips.

CJ chuckles. I know she thinks MJ is outrageous at times, but I can tell we're all in agreement with her assessment of Michael. I admit to myself that he's a 10, but I'm not starting that conversation with MJ.

'Can you lot contain yourselves, please?' I sing out as Angel walks into the building carrying a box marked 'fragile'.

Once inside, CJ, Angel, and I take a conveyor-belt approach to the glasses, cutlery, and dinner set, and it's all washed and dried in my tiny kitchen in record time while MJ tackles a box marked 'STUFF'. It's cosy and familiar as we move easily around each other with the intimacy of partners gliding around a dancefloor. I smile to myself when I notice we're also all colour-coordinated with the black-and-white splashback tiles.

I'm facing the sink overlooking the street and turn quickly to see CJ placing the rest of the coffee mugs, handles to the left, on the shelf near the fridge, while Angel arranges the cutlery like she has in her own home, and MJ considers every knick-knack she unpacks before placing them on the breakfast bar by size. All of us methodical in our own ways, similar ways.

This is the first time I've thought of moving as fun. I love being back with the women who know me best. We've always been there for house-moves, boyfriend break-ups, sorry business, and just for coffee and yarns. We do life together and having them here as I resettle makes it that much easier to move on from the mess I left in Sydney.

'Hey, what's this?' MJ holds up a black satin bag and starts laughing.

'Oh, that's Charles!' I chuckle at CJ's look of absolute horror. 'Don't panic, I didn't mince him up and put him in there. It's my vibrator, I call him Charles. Remember that fella about five years ago? Still the best shag I've ever had. So, ladies, meet Charles #2!'

I take the bag from MJ, put Charles aside, and change the subject. 'While we're all together, can we sort your birthday, CJ? It's only a month away. What do you want to do?'

CJ takes a deep breath, looking left and right as if we're in a public space and she's about to divulge top-secret national security data. 'I want to go to a rodeo,' she whispers.

MJ lets out a loud, 'Yee-ha!' and does some weird bowlegged movement, kicking her feet up as if she's line dancing and river dancing at the same time. 'Rodeos mean cowboys, so count me in.'

At first there's excitement in Angel's eyes. She loves live country music, like lots of Murris do. But then she starts to frown. I'm guessing that she's thinking about animal cruelty at the rodeo, so before the moment spirals into awkwardness, I say, 'I'll go with, but we need to talk about animal cruelty at some point.' I look at my cousin and she nods in agreement, as do the others.

I'm desperate to ask CJ why she wants to go to a rodeo, though I don't want to sound judgemental. Angel's pointed out that character flaw of mine more than once over the years. I like to consider myself as an observationist, rather than a judgementalist. As no-one else is forthcoming with the question, I dive in. 'But why, for the love of god, do you want to go to a rodeo?'

'*Don't* judge me!' CJ warns. 'If you're going to judge me, then I won't tell you.'

I try to reassure her. 'We're the coven of non-judgemental witches, you know that.'

CJ clears her throat, looks around again, and mutters, 'The thing is, I've always wanted to be with a cowboy.'

MJ laughs out loud. 'And you all reckon *I'm* outrageous! We need more bubbly.'

I can't stop laughing as I try to pour the last of the

now-warm champagne into our mugs. CJ frowns. It's obvious that she doesn't see anything funny about the moment, and I feel bad. I know how sensitive she is. I sit down next to her on the floor and throw my arm around her shoulder.

'It's *always* the quiet ones,' I tell her. 'Our perfect, hardworking public schoolteacher, marching for better conditions, lover of literature, marker of essays, tutor of overachieving students.'

Angel holds her mug up in a toast and continues the list. 'Patron of the drama club and the debating team, always academic, prim, and proper.'

MJ takes a sip of bubbly, then finishes, 'All the while, secretly fantasising about shagging a cowboy. Gotta love that.'

Angel grabs the ukulele that arrived in my 'fragile' box, starts to pluck the strings, and mumbles some words by Kasey Chambers about wanting a cowboy when she grows up.

CJ tilts her head, smiling coyly as MJ snaps photos then films Angel, all to be uploaded to Instagram stories before the day is out. She's a deadly freelance photographer, and honestly, with her healthy following on her socials, she's never really off the clock.

'So there *is* a rodeo in Warwick on my birthday weekend,' CJ tells us. 'If you're all keen, I can organise an itinerary and all the logistics.' Her face is hopeful, enthusiastic.

'Like a school excursion,' I laugh, 'but without the annoying kids.'

She jumps to her feet. 'Exactly! I can book the tickets and accommodation, you just need to get your outfits.'

'Outfits?' I repeat in mock outrage. 'You won't *ever* see me in blinged jeans, fringed boots or a cowboy hat!' I touch my hair. 'I spend too much on my hair to cover it up.'

Angel eyeballs me.

'Oh, right,' I scoff at my cousin. 'And I can just see *you* in a checked or chambray muumuu, with fringes on your crocs.'

Angel grins at CJ as if my sarcasm has given her inspiration for her wardrobe. She uncrosses her legs, spreads them out fully in front of her, and proudly rolls her croc-ed feet left to right. 'According to social media, I am fun and fashionable and these classic platform crocs are the most popular, so there!'

The truth is that I love how my cousin is totally comfortable in her skin and her wardrobe. But Angel is also a vegan and always worrying about animal cruelty, so I don't know how she's going to cope with the rodeo adventure. Before I have the chance to ask, there's a knock at the door.

It's Michael from upstairs. I know he's the kind of guy MJ would love to throw to the ground and crawl all over, but that might be a weird first impression to make with my new neighbour. I walk over to open the screen door before she can get up.

'I didn't mean to interrupt,' he says in that gorgeous voice. 'I just thought you might like some herbs. A little welcome-to-the-building gift.' He hands me some cuttings and I notice again the muscles in his forearms. 'I grow them on my balcony and always have plenty, if you ever need any.' I'm now also noticing that he smells good. Or rather, as MJ would say, he smells *delicious*; there's a hint of lavender and spicy cinnamon and vanilla. I know it's not the herbs I can smell, because this scent is wearable *and* expensive.

'Thank you.' I look at the basil, rosemary, and mint and realise that I have zero food in the flat, and a big, boring grocery shop awaits. I'll need to get to the markets on the weekend for my fruit and veg.

There's an awkward pause, and I can feel everyone staring at me. I look at Michael. 'Sorry, we were just in the middle of planning something when you knocked.' I don't know why I feel uncomfortable, but I'd rather he didn't linger.

'Oh right, of course.' He's already moving away from the door. 'Sorry to interrupt. Hope you ladies have a nice day, and good luck with your planning,' he says politely, before heading back up the stairwell.

'See you later, thanks for the herbs, very kind of you!' I sing out after him, feeling that my manners are lacking.

'You could've invited him in,' Angel suggests.

'I don't even know him,' I point out. 'I don't really want him checking out my apartment.'

'He carried your books up, brought you herbs. I'm fairly sure he's just being a good neighbour,' she replies. 'Sydney's made you very suspicious.'

'I'm not a suspicious person, I'm a private person. I don't want a man I've known for three seconds in my home. I don't *need* any men in my home. I've got Charles and he'll do for now. If I need to get laid, I'll do it the old-fashioned way and go to the pub on Friday night,' I joke. I pick the herbs up and take them to the sink, but I can see in my periphery that MJ is shaking her head, appalled at how slack I am at recognising a good thing literally on my doorstep.

I sit back down on the floor with the others, pick up my mug and hold it in a toast. 'Here's to being here with you, to my new home, to my dream job, and to my fresh herbs. I believe my life is now complete!'

# CHAPTER TWO

'Wow, when you said you'd do an itinerary, you weren't kidding!' I laugh. MJ and Angel are also inspecting our personalised laminated, spiral-bound schedules, all prepared and hand-delivered by CJ. We're sitting below the pergola in Angel's backyard which overlooks a sizeable veggie patch of pumpkin, snake beans, chillis, capsicums, and anything else she can grow in the heat of the Brisbane summer and share with the neighbours of her Queenslander.

I read the cover of CJ's itinerary: *Rodeo Dreaming*. I'm thinking *Cowboy Crawl* might be a more appropriate title. Every group needs an organiser and CJ is ours. She's been thorough in her preparation: there's an aerial map, weblinks, hotel information, and a 'What to bring' list, including rodeo dress-ups, boots, long pants, and running gear. 'Thanks for putting something for me in there, CJ.'

CJ beams with pride as we turn page after page. The sun is setting and bats glide across the mauve sky as they always do at dusk. Darkness swoops in quickly behind the bats. Angel lights some candles while I light some insect coils before we're all eaten alive.

'Ugg boot shopping? Is that for me?' Angel asks, and CJ nods.

'They're like winter crocs for you, right, cuz?' I joke, and she nods and winks.

'What about me? Is there anything in the itinerary for me?' MJ pouts and pretends to be wounded at being left out.

'The wineries are for you, MJ!' CJ pats MJ's hand and MJ laughs.

'You've outdone yourself, sis,' she says.

'Thank you.' CJ stands and takes a bow. 'It's the teacher in me. I do have the most organised class at Green Bank High School.'

'Hang on.' I reach for my wine. 'How come on the Saturday night we're all staying in cabins, and you're staying at the Buckaroo Hotel? Is it a better hotel? Because if it is, then I'm staying there, too.'

Angel rolls her eyes and mouths 'snob' at me, and I put my palm up to her face.

'She's staying at the Buckaroo in case she gets a fuckaroo, right?' MJ laughs and swigs a mouthful of wine as if it's lemonade.

CJ doesn't deny MJ's allegation. 'It's been a long time since I've been between the sheets with a fella, so I'm hoping I can kill two birds with my birthday plan.'

Angel gives CJ a tight side-hug. 'I hope you'll find your own Kev soon.'

As if on cue, Kev appears with his pushbike. He's sweaty from the ride home, so he just blows kisses to us all before placing a box of treats on the table. 'Thought you might like some of these choc hazelnut buckwheat balls.'

'CJ will take the bucken balls.' MJ keels over laughing and we join in like schoolgirls.

Kev looks confused. 'You women are all crazy,' he says, kissing Angel quickly on the top of her head. She leans up into it like a happy cat. Then Kev props his bike against the fence and heads back into the darkness of the garden that leads to their house.

'Okay, okay, enough carry-on. I need to get my wardrobe sorted. Who's coming shopping with me?' CJ picks up a buckwheat ball and chuckles again. 'I need blinged jeans, a checked shirt, a *big* belt buckle, and boots. I need it all. I probably need some lingerie, too. I should make a list.' She pulls her phone out and starts a list in Notes.

'I'm not buying blinged jeans,' I announce, 'but I know the rules. One in, all in.'

\* \* \*

A few days later, I return from my morning run, panting as if I've never run before. I'm conscious that I really need to get my fitness levels up after months of little or no exercise. I miss being in top form, so I take the stairs to my flat, so focussed on the running stats on my smartwatch that it's not until the last minute that I notice that Michael is also in the stairwell, heading out. I'm all sweaty, hot, and messy, which makes him look even better in his grey marle suit, white shirt, navy tie, and patent black shoes.

'Looking flash,' I say, then feel a bit embarrassed. I hope he doesn't think I'm flirting with him.

Michael pauses and laughs warmly. 'Oh, I'm just going to work. But if you're keen for company, I'll run with you of a morning, or walk if you'd prefer to yarn.'

I remember what Angel said about Sydney making me suspicious, so I smile and reply before my natural caution pulls me back. 'Sure, a walk and yarn would be great on my non-run days. I need some help getting back in form, but I hope I can keep up with you.'

Michael continues down the stairs to the carpark. 'Great, I'll pop in later to organise a time,' he calls over his shoulder.

I make a point of being at my kitchen window as he pulls out of the driveway in his white Tesla. I peer through the venetian blinds like the neighbourhood gossip. That suited, fancy-car Murri might be good value as a neighbour, especially because it never hurt to have a handsome, potential plus-one living nearby, since Charles was only fit for the bedroom.

With ABC Breakfast on in the background, I cringe at the news of yet another copyright infringement on a First Nations artist whose work has been reproduced on dodgy tea towels at a local market. I shower, dress, and, with a sense of purpose, head into the Gallery of First Nations

Art on the fringes of the city. I love my new workplace, known to most as GoFNA. I'm really enjoying working with the small team of passionate staff who have been transforming what was part of an old coffee chain into a functioning gallery and event space. With our small but supportive governing committee, I feel like this is going to be the best career move of my life. The silver lining of the fiasco down south is that my new role here recognises my skills and expertise, and allows me both freedom and growth in a way that the Sydney scene didn't.

As I walk through the space, I imagine the grand opening in August. I visualise small pieces of art hanging in the manager's office, one wall dedicated purely to southeast Queensland artists, a shop selling an ever-growing First Nations wearable art range, plus weavings, and handmade jewellery from across the country.

The pizza kitchen across the lane fires up their oven way before lunchtime and my mouth waters while I examine my jampacked schedule for the day: several zoom calls, writing funding applications, an informal check-in with a philanthropist, and dedicated time to researching the artists who will appear in my first exhibition for the gallery.

It's a long, productive day with few interruptions, and by 7 pm, I've managed to work through most of my to-do list. I'm still at my desk and my stomach is grumbling loudly. As I flick through the portfolio of an artist I've not heard of before, I have an 'a-ha' moment, forcing me to sit upright. Daniel Davies, from Warwick, only a couple of hours drive from Magandjin. He's been pitched by his representative as the 'Namatjira of the Southern Downs'. I take in Davies' landscapes with a keen eye. I like that they offer something extra, a story with a message about Australia's environmental climate crisis, with millennia worth of local knowledge woven into the canvases. There are phrases emblazoned on each artwork – enviroTORMENT, CLIMATE CRIES-IS, ACT OR DIE – DO YOU CARE? – challenging the viewer to consider their own role.

I sit back, contemplating this new exciting artwork, trying to define his style. His political landscapes look to me like Gordon Hookey-meets-Blak Douglas-meets-Namatjira. I email the staff and committee to invite their feedback, saying, 'May not be to everyone's taste, but it doesn't have to be. This work is fresh, meaningful, challenging, topical. Davies also works with young people, so we could potentially have school groups visit and utilise the vacant office upstairs for workshops.' I hit send and feel a sense of achievement, like this moment is the beginning of something significant for the gallery, for the artist, and for me.

I know I should get home, but I want to know more about this fella. Time ticks by as I scroll through page after page online, reading about Davies and his personal life.

It appears the committee are all working late as well. Supportive emails come in one after the other, encouraging me to meet with Davies and potentially weave him into the proposed exhibition. I'm excited at the thought of connecting with him. It's only then that I realise he lives literally minutes from where we're going for CJ's birthday weekend. My interest in the rodeo road trip is definitely on the rise.

To my surprise, a bottle of pinot noir awaits me on my doorstep when I arrive home, exhausted, at 9 pm. There's a note on the back of a business card:

*A gift from a client, but I don't drink red, thought you might like it. Text me if you want to walk or run in the morning before work. X Michael*

I read the note again when I get inside, thinking the X is odd for a near-stranger, but put his number into my phone as I've done with the other neighbours I've met since I settled in. I pour a glass of the wine, kick off my heels, and sit on the couch. Netflix offers some company as I try to relax, still wired with the anticipation of snagging Daniel Davies for the gallery. Hoping it's not too late, I text Michael:

Hi, hope I'm not waking you, just home. Walk in the morning would be great. What time?

The phone is barely out of my hand when it beeps with a reply.

Hey! Didn't wake me. Just reading. Meet you downstairs at 6 am. Night.

I respond:

Cool. And thank you for the wine. Dinner!

At 5.45 am, my alarm rings and I spring out of bed. The sun is streaming in my kitchen window, and it's already hot as I ruefully remember the almond croissant I shovelled down the day before and the wine I had for dinner. All that sugar makes me crazy but I still do it. I'm surprised I'm not hungover with so little food in my belly. I pull on my running shorts and shoes, run a brush through my hair and some toothpaste across my front teeth, and head down to meet Michael, who is stretching his calves as I reach the front gate. When he turns and sees me, a broad, almost-perfect smile forms across his face and I can't help but smile back. I wish I'd cleaned my teeth properly.

'*Every* woman needs a Michael in their life for early morning exercise,' I tell him, grateful for the added motivation to my running. It's always better and easier to work out with others. I almost bounce to the front gate.

'You seem happy,' he says.

'Best time of the day. Which way?' I ask.

'Which way, what?'

'Which direction?' I laugh. It's easy to be around this fella, even at 6 am.

'Let's go down that way, then take the hill?'

I don't really want to take any hills because of the vino-dinner, but I smile and agree because I also don't want to waste time and energy thinking about an alternative route.

I run for my mental health most days. While running with a hangover is a punishment, life is a balance, and there are some dining choices that are worth taking hills for. I'm grateful just to have someone to get me out of bed on the more difficult days.

'How long have you lived here?' I ask, realising this is our first real conversation. We move to a steady pace as Michael tells me he's been in Magandjin for five years but is originally from Cairns.

'I moved to Sydney to study,' he says. 'Stayed longer than I wanted to because work took over, but I'm happy to be back in the Sunshine State.'

'Did you enjoy the nightlife in Sydney? It's a bit quieter here in Magandjin.' I'm not sure why I ask him this – I'm not a clubber myself.

It seems we have more things in common in addition to running, because Michael echoes my thoughts. 'I'm not a big clubber really. I much prefer a nice restaurant and the arts. What about you?' he asks. 'What brings you here?'

I'm not sure I should tell him I moved back because I kind of got run out of town. I keep it basic: mob, current job, hobbies. 'I'm Wiradyuri but grew up here. Also moved to Sydney for work. I work in the arts.' I pause to catch my breath, while Michael appears to be focussing on his strides.

'And now?' he asks when he notices I've slowed a bit.

'Oh, now I'm curator at the Gallery of First Nations Art, in the cultural precinct. We're opening in August. You should come to opening night.'

'I'd love that. I've collected a couple of pieces from artists that speak to me,' he says. 'Let me know the date and I'll lock it in my diary.' He suddenly stretches an arm out right across my body, blocking me from stepping off the curb. As if he has some sixth sense, a dark green SUV comes flying around the corner.

'Whoa, thanks.' I take a step back.

'No time for ambos and hospitals today, we've got another three Ks to go,' he jokes, leading us across the now-safe road.

For the rest of the walk, I tell Michael about my family, my favourite artists, why the gallery is such a significant place for our mob. The space is about confidence, conviction, and truth-telling. When I say it out loud, I feel empowered, like I've come alive.

Michael tells me he loves the river life and being able to exercise outdoors all year round in Magandjin. 'I go to the gym *occasionally*,' he says with a laugh. We also have that in common.

When I tell him about the pending rodeo road trip to Warwick, we laugh about rhinestones and fringes and men in chaps. I notice how intently he listens, asking questions, and making the most of the conversation about me. While I'm conscious of hogging the limelight, I really do love talking about my work. I mentally resolve to ask Michael more about his work during our next walk.

\*\*\*

The following Saturday, I'm heavily caffeinated as CJ, MJ, Angel, and I stroll along Latrobe Terrace in Paddington. CJ leads the way with her op-shopping itinerary. There's laughter and the occasional outburst of country singing by Angel, but I find myself dawdling a bit. To be honest, I'm not really that interested in the shopping, and I'm quietly trying to work out how to manage the humidity frizzing up my newly cut-and-coloured hair, and still thinking about the phone calls I didn't get to make at work yesterday.

CJ is banging on about a shop with amazing shirts and another store across the road with great jeans. We follow her in and out of thrift shops, each one allegedly more interesting than the last.

'Ta-da!' She steps out of one changeroom in full rodeo regalia, but barefoot. An assistant hands her a pair of cowgirl boots that have a tinge of pink to them, insisting that CJ needs them to complete her outfit. CJ screws up her nose, politely taking the boots from the young woman. 'I really don't want to stand out.'

I burst out laughing. 'Stand out?! Let's just look at you, Tidda.' I spin her around and we all huddle in front of the full-length mirror in the middle of the store. 'Hat, tick. Chambray shirt. Tick. The biggest, blingiest belt buckle this side of Mt Isa. Biggest tick!' I spin CJ around again and bend her over slightly so her butt is pointing towards the mirror. 'And the pièce de resistance, I'd say, is the bedazzled arse!' By now we're all busting ourselves laughing. 'If you think it's going to take the *boots* to make you stand out, then I'm sorry, CJ, you are more than slightly misguided.'

It's the most I've laughed in ages. Moments like these make me the happiest to be back with my sistagirls.

'Stop it, I'm going to pee my pants,' CJ says, cross-legged.

Angel eyes CJ up and down, waving her hand towards the boots. 'I love this look. The boots set the whole scene for your story.'

MJ agrees, snapping a pic for Instagram, and adds it to the Rodeo Dreaming hashtag she's set up for us to follow for the weekend.

The sales assistant confirms that CJ is rodeo-ready, then looks at me and declares that I need help. She attempts to hand me a checked shirt, mumbling something about how it will look good on me. I'm going to need more caffeine – or wine – to get through this.

I throw the shirt on over my singlet. As the assistant steps in to help, I shoo her away. 'I think I can tuck myself in, thanks.'

She cautiously suggests tying it in front, nervously stepping in to assist again, then moves away.

I turn to the mirror. It actually looks okay as I twist left and right to gauge the different angles.

'You look hot, you know you do.' MJ says, taking a photo. 'Put this on Insta, it's a thirst-trap for sure.'

I try to get MJ's phone off her, half laughing. 'I'll leave the thirst-trapping to you, thanks very much.' I get out of the shirt faster than I got into it and turn to CJ. 'Is it lunchtime on your schedule? All this shopping has worked up my appetite.'

CJ looks at her watch and nods. 'Almost. Table's been booked for 12.30.'

I'm happy the shopping is over so we can sit and chill for a while. CJ announces that we're going to go through the updated itinerary for the rodeo during lunch. She's apparently made some additions to our program.

'Of course you have,' I giggle. 'I may need you to organise my life.'

Within minutes, we are seated, food is ordered, and shopping bargains are being looked at one more time. The energy is high and the mood bright. This is how I want to spend my downtime, eating and enjoying the day with my besties.

'Right, I know some of you don't want to be at the rodeo the *whole* time.' CJ hands out the latest draft of the itinerary.

'How about *any* of the time, is that an option?' I snark. Angel nudges me. 'Sorry, I'll stop being a downer.' But as CJ and MJ admire each other's belt buckles, I murmur to her, 'Why aren't *you* saying anything? You're the one who texted me about the RSPCA being opposed to rodeos because of the "potential for significant injury, suffering, or distress to the animals involved".'

Angel shakes her head, and I can see my cousin is conflicted. 'What do you want me to do?' she replies quietly. 'This is what she wants for her birthday and we're her best friends. I don't love the thought of rodeos, but I do love CJ, so, I'll keep my mouth shut for as long as I can morally do so. I think it would be nice if you did, too. You're *almost* a vegan.'

'How dare you!' I feign offence. 'Veganism is a colonial construct. If anything, I'm a pseudo-vegetarian because I eat roo. Our Ancestors and our mob still eat meat – roo, emu . . .'

I can see Angel wants to say more, but CJ has taken charge of the table. 'There's an amazing food trail I found,' she says, flipping to that page in the itinerary. 'You can buy local produce there, Angel. Apples are big in the area, so is cider, pie, and the like.'

It's cute to see Angel's eyes widen with excitement. 'Kev told me there's also somewhere we can pick our own strawberries. And there's truffles and cheese.'

'But you don't eat cheese!' I point out.

'I know, but *you* girls do. And who knows? They may have some vegan cheese there.' She has an answer for everything and I can't help but love her for it.

'I'm going to need those wineries if there's vegan cheese on this trip,' MJ jokes.

'Speaking of wine and cheese, that fella from upstairs dropped off a bottle of wine the other night,' I tell them. 'It was on the doorstep when I got home – he said he doesn't drink red. We went for a walk the next morning.' I speak matter-of-factly, but anyone would think I'd announced I was running for president at the level of interest from the girls. I shake my head and wish I'd not said anything at all. 'I really don't know what to make of him,' I admit. 'But he seems like a nice guy. We're going to start walking to the markets on Saturday mornings for our fruit and veg, too.'

'Walking dates, love it,' MJ says. 'I reckon you could have some fun with that one.' She raises her eyebrows as she photographs the food on the table. 'He's clearly interested.'

'I don't see anything romantic happening, but it's good to have some male energy in my day.'

The others roll their eyes and shake their heads, as much in disappointment as disbelief. I know they all think he's gorgeous, and of course he is. But what I need right now is friends, not another potential man-disaster. I think I'm pretty good at blocking out the stuff I don't need.

'I can see you mob,' I say, sipping my coffee. 'Don't roll your eyes at me. I'm just saying that with you lot and most of the gallery staff also being deadly young women, you do notice the gap in male energy. But that's the only gap I want filled right now!' I laugh and fork up some salad. 'I know you all think the best way to get over a man is to get under another one, but I'm already over what happened in Sydney. I have Michael to exercise with in the morning, and Charles to keep me company of a night, and what I really need now is to focus on my new job and cementing myself here in the Queensland art scene. It's my love affair with the gallery I need your encouragement on, and it's the only love affair I want right now, okay?'

MJ's not quite ready to let it go. 'I wouldn't write him off too soon. Herbs, wine, walking. I'd be tapping that Murri, no questions asked,' she says with a laugh.

'Then go for it,' I suggest. 'I'm happy to have him as my neighbour, but that's it.' I smile as MJ rubs her hands together with a cartoonishly villainous look on her face.

CJ and Angel ask a string of questions about Michael. I answer as quickly as I can so we can get this conversation done with. 'He's an architect, he drives a Tesla, he's fit, he's into the arts. He's originally from Cairns, he doesn't drink red, prefers a bubbly. And yes, he's pretty easy on the eye.' I don't tell them that he's also an incredibly good listener because they'll have me married up in no time.

MJ repeats Michael's profile: tall, dark, handsome Murri, with a gorgeous smile. She makes a sexy grunting noise. 'I am *more* than happy to take one for the team.'

I move the conversation along. 'In other news, I've got a meeting with a young Murri artist near the rodeo. Could be a real game-changer if I can get him for the gallery. I need the gallery opening to really make a splash and kick off my working life in Magandjin with a bang. I think this artist in Warwick can help make that happen. On top of that, I'm worried that the legacy of why I left Sydney is following me, and I need to shake it if I'll ever be fully confident in the arts space again.'

Angel puts her hand on mine and warmly says, 'You will make a splash, wow everyone, and be back at the top of your game, cuz. And we'll be beside you every step of the way.'

# CHAPTER THREE

'What the hell have you got in here, CJ? We're only going for two nights.' I struggle to get CJ's case into the already-packed boot of my car.

As she straightens her Akubra, CJ lists off what she's packed, which includes – but is not limited to – three pairs of boots, four pairs of jeans, two checked shirts, one pair of Daisy Dukes, a white singlet, a black singlet, and lingerie. As if that's not enough, she's also packed her running gear because MJ said there may be a cowboy in Lycra, but also because she thinks *I* might like to do the Park Run. Her excitement is just too precious.

'Thanks for suggesting the running, CJ, but have you considered that maybe I want to run *away* from you lot for an hour on Saturday morning?' I quip. The girls giggle as they climb into the car, and the fun begins.

The drive from Magandjin to Warwick is as entertaining as Angel can make it, her guitar resting across her and MJ's laps. The roof of my convertible is down, and MJ entertains herself by taking photos and videos along the way, uploading to Instagram and TikTok as she goes.

As we pass lavender fields, it feels wonderfully freeing to be going away with my tiddas for the weekend, a freedom that the busyness of Sydney never really afforded me. I'll have to do some work when meeting Daniel Davies, but other than that, it's just us girls on an adventure. I smile from the inside out, finally starting to feel in control of my life after the turmoil of the previous year.

'Sweet baby cheeses,' CJ says as a truck rushes past. 'That's got to be the 10th semi to scare the living daylights out of me. Angel, can you play something? I need a distraction.'

Angel never needs to be asked twice to play or sing, and within seconds, she is strumming along to an old Kenny Rogers number and the entire car are belting out an old favourite.

It reminds me of the late Aunty Ruby Langford Ginibi's memoir, *Don't Take Your Love to Town*, which we all read at school. Aunt's work was groundbreaking in publishing back then, pushing her editors not to gubbarise her text. Her authenticity in storytelling is what inspires me when curating exhibitions. It's that same authenticity in Daniel Davies' paintings which he challenges the viewers of his work with.

Angel is singing every line word- and pitch-perfect, and I make a mental note to ask her to sing at the gallery opening. I always love to showcase local talent whenever

I can, though I'm conscious of it being a conflict of interest. I'll get the board to sign off on it just to be transparent.

By the time we arrive at Warwick, we've sung along to the best of Kenny and Patsy Cline, but I think we need to update the playlist. 'I'm choosing the music on the way home,' I insist, looking at Angel in the rearview mirror. 'And it'll be Troy Cassar-Daley, Nardi Simpson, and Frank Yamma!'

'Can I have a say? It *is* my birthday weekend,' CJ pipes up.

'Of course, darling. What would the birthday girl like, other than a birthday bonk?' MJ cackles as she passes a bag around to gather all the road trip food wrappers from the near two-hour drive.

CJ thinks a minute. 'I'd like some Jimmy Little and Uncle Bobby Randall, please. They were true country gentlemen and I'd say they'd be fitting acknowledgement for our rodeo weekend.'

\*\*\*

I'm due to meet Daniel Davies ten minutes after we finish lunch. 'It's not far from here, so I'll walk to the gallery to meet him,' I tell the girls. 'You take the car and I'll see you back at the hotel later.' I hand CJ the keys. 'Maybe we can get a swim in. It's so bloody hot here.'

While waiting for Daniel to arrive, I walk through the permanent exhibition where a few of his pieces hang. He's won the Regional Art Gallery Prize for a mixed media piece – photography and acrylic – and by the space devoted to his work, he appears to be something of a local celebrity. When Daniel enters the gallery, I'm a little taken aback. I'm more careful than ever to maintain a professional position with artists, but I can't help but notice his lean frame, high cheekbones, dark, smouldering brown eyes, and incredible smile. Daniel Davies is a bone fide hottie.

After a slightly awkward handshake, we sit on a couch in the foyer and I invite him to tell me a little more about himself.

He tells me he is one of the local mob and they've been here for millennia. It's his own connection to Country that inspires his work, whether it appears obvious on the canvas or not.

'Oh, it's obvious to me,' I say, my curatorial hat well and truly on. 'Your connection to Country, your challenge to viewers, your calls to action around the climate crisis, are all so important in the world today.'

He nods and waits for my next question, which surprises me. Most of the artists I've worked with have been more than happy to sit and talk about themselves and their work without any prompts from me at all. Daniel seems a little more reserved, so I swiftly dig my notebook from my bag and start with his background. 'Are there many artists in your family?'

He gives a deep laugh. 'No, I'm the only "artist".' He does air quotes. 'That's how my family, especially my brother, describe me to others. In fact, he might even support those Extinction Rebellion protestors gluing themselves to my paintings in the hope of ruining them.'

I chuckle at that, but I catch myself immediately when Daniel appears to be serious. I'm intrigued and want to know about his story, delve deeper. It turns out that Daniel's family are cattle people, stockmen and women, and he's apparently the black sheep of the family. I want to know how Blackfellas become cattle people when cattle do so much damage to the land and are significant greenhouse gas producers contributing to climate change. Understanding the themes of Daniel's work, I can also understand why he's regarded as the black sheep. Daniel starts to relax and open up.

'You'll have to talk to *them* about cattle,' he says, 'because I don't understand it either.' He tells me he's an environmentalist, concerned for animal welfare. His family support him, but he feels like he stands out like a sore thumb because he reads poetry, is a painter, and likes to spend time with intellectual, arty women. 'Maybe I've ostracised myself,' he says. He stands, so I stand too. He takes a deep breath, picks up a brochure from the plinth next to him, and shares more without any prompting. 'My family, except for my sister, see my art about the environment and social justice as *too* political. And my brother, well, he isn't . . . how can I say this . . . we're like chalk and cheese. But we all have a role to play in our families, don't we, Annie?'

I hate my name being shortened, but all I need to do today is form a connection in the hope that we can secure his talent and work for GoFNA. *Suck it up, Annie*, I tell myself.

We spend the next hour talking about my proposal for the gallery opening. Daniel talks about his own vision for exhibiting his work and shows me some new pieces in his portfolio, and we plan to meet at GoFNA in the weeks ahead.

My phone rings as we're walking out. It's CJ.

'I better take this,' I say. 'Might be an emergency.'

It's not, of course. It turns out CJ wants to tell me that the rodeo museum they're at is very interesting. 'I'm just finishing up,' I tell her. 'I'll be there in 10.' I end the call and apologise to Daniel. 'The girls want me to meet them at the rodeo museum.'

Daniel waves off the apology. 'I can drop you there, if you like? It's on the way to my next stop.'

'Thanks, I won't say no to that,' I reply with a smile. 'The humidity is killing me!'

When we arrive a few minutes later, my tiddas are out front, taking selfies. They stop when they see us, looking impressed at Daniel's metallic green Holden ute with his artwork adorning the doors. MJ is by my side in seconds, pulling her camera out and lining up a shot. Daniel loves the attention and leans against the car in a casual pose. The guy definitely knows how gorgeous he is.

'We need a selfie,' MJ motions the girls to get close to Daniel and the car, and she takes about 10 photos before Daniel pulls away.

'I need to get some art supplies while I'm in town,' he says, grinning. 'It was great meeting you, Annie.'

I shake his hand, this time not so awkwardly. 'Let's talk during the week. I'll get onto your management and get the ball rolling.'

Daniel leans in, gives me a peck on the cheek, then he pecks the others as well, who blush like schoolgirls. As we stand under the heat of the afternoon sun, they wait for the travelling artwork to turn the corner before they start to grill me.

'You *hate* being called Annie,' CJ declares. 'But he was a gentleman and clearly talented, so we'll forgive him that small error.'

MJ's not having any talk of talent and gentlemanly behaviour, preferring to focus on, in her words, the 'freaking hotness of Daniel'. 'You have *got* to date him,' she says as we walk into the air-conditioned rodeo museum.

I shut that line of thinking down firmly. 'Listen, MJ, I was let down in Sydney, unfairly and wrongly judged. I'm not giving even a *hint* of an opportunity for the arts community to betray me again. Even if Daniel *is* the hottest thing since Dan Sultan.'

'Fair enough. Maybe I should take a crack at Daniel myself. I like them tall and lean. I should add that to my Tinder profile,' she laughs and licks her lips.

\* \* \*

As we walk into the hotel bistro, CJ suggests we should stay late for karaoke.

'You mean Koori-oke, or Murri-oke seeing as we're in Queensland!' I say, looking around the country pub with zero intention of singing.

Angel is excited, though, and squeals, 'I'm in!'

I pull her in for a hug and kiss her on the cheek. 'You're more like scary-oke.'

While we wait for dinner, MJ shows us her op shop bargains from the day, including a frilly black dress she scored for $5.

'I can see you shaking your booty in that in the Valley,' I smile. MJ grins back cheekily. We all know what she's like on a night out.

CJ has her itinerary out, rattling off the walks around town and the riverfront, and the sculptures of a platypus and one of Tiddalik by Vern Foss.

MJ actually spits her wine across the table. She chuckles, wiping her face on Angel's arms. 'I don't mean to be disrespectful, but I'm up for a tidda-lick.' And like a bunch of schoolgirls, we crack up laughing.

\* \* \*

I rise early with the sun. I love waking in a new place and seeing the landscape at dawn. I pull on my activewear and head to the river for a run, passing locals out for morning walks, and take in the lush landscape after what appears to be recent rain. I think about my own Country back in Wagga Wagga and the Marrambidya Bila, laughing to myself about what locals call the Wagga Beach. I miss my miyagan and the BBQs and catch-ups they often have on the weekends. I don't know when I'll get back down there again, but the Aunties and Uncles are always asking when I'll be back. It's just such a long trip if I can't get a direct flight.

I take a deep breath and close my eyes for a second, then look at this landscape that reminds me a little of my own Country, and I feel a pang of guilt about not going home enough, as much as I want to, as much as I should. I tell myself to make the most of the beauty around me today. My friends and my work are important too, and at least today I can be somewhere that looks a little like my own ngurrambang.

I run for about a kilometre, then slow my pace to stare at the river gums in front of me. I take my earbuds out and walk to one of the trees. I get in as close as I can, wrap my arms around its trunk, and hug tightly.

'Leave some love for someone who may need it later,' my late-Nanna Sony told me as a child. A lone tear runs down my cheek as I remember when I was at my lowest in Sydney after the scandal broke. Nanna was no longer with us by then, and I missed her so much during that time. The hardest thing since she passed over has been not being able to yarn with her whenever I want to. I hadn't even been able to find a tree to hug, to draw extra love from. As I step back from the gum, I hope the love I leave today will help someone else later.

When I put my earbuds back in, my phone pings with a message from CJ:

Where are you? Itinerary says breakfast is at 7. We're at the café next door to the hotel. I've ordered you a Zymil latte. Be dressed by 8.30 to leave by 9.30 xo

I shake my head, smiling, and reply:

Just out running, so I don't have to Park Run tomorrow. There shortly, start eating without me xo

I know the actual rodeo proper doesn't start till the evening, so I'm not in a rush, and I'm not sure why we have to spend the entire day at the showground with all the dust and animal smells. I'm not going to complain, though, because CJ has always been one of the most thoughtful people I know, even if she's a tad obsessed with her schedule. I also know that collectively our group is probably like herding cats and we should probably give her a medal for getting us here at all. I turn around and head to the car, promising to give my tidda the attention she deserves on her birthday weekend.

# CHAPTER FOUR

'Oh. My. God. You look amazing!' I can't believe how incredible CJ looks as she steps out of her motel room and does a little boot-scoot along the verandah. 'Do that again so MJ can put it on TikTok.'

MJ's already capturing it all. I am so inspired by CJ's transformation into rodeo queen, I've got Nancy Sinatra in my head, but I'm not embarrassing myself by attempting to sing.

'And look at you!' I turn to Angel, who is decked out in a chambray muumuu and boots. She tries to pirouette but almost falls over. 'Is that leather on your feet?' I ask cheekily.

Angel is disgusted at the suggestion. 'Of course not! They're *pleather*. Kev got them for me and he loaned me his Akubra. I think it works.'

'It really does. You look great!' I say. 'You're an eco-rodeo queen.'

'And what about you, MJ?' Angel says.

'Those cut-offs will definitely attract the cowboys,' I laugh. 'I don't think it's just sistagirl CJ who we need to get laid this weekend.' I'm surprised by how much I'm enjoying the dress-ups, and I'm actually getting excited about heading to the rodeo with my besties.

When we arrive at the showground, I focus on finding a park while CJ re-reads the program for the day out loud. MJ insists we start with a selfie in front of the rodeo sign. The anticipation is killing CJ, though, and she surges ahead through the entrance. MJ follows close behind, filming every step.

As we enter the turnstiles, we move in slightly different directions, soaking up all that's on offer. There's a sea of men in Ariat shirts and Wranglers, big belt buckles, cowboy boots, and Akubras of all colours. CJ is already looking around with intent, but I think she'll be looking for a while, because at a first glance, there are only young and retired riders here, nothing or no-one too inspiring in our age range.

MJ commentates as she films, 'Here we are, your first rodeo, *our* first rodeo! Happy birthday, CJ.'

CJ spins around and smiles into MJ's iPhone. 'I need to see *everything*,' she says seriously and takes off.

There's a mix of carnival tunes, country music, and a commentator over the loudspeaker, but it's not chaotic. Not yet, anyway. CJ's excitement is palpable. She's walking and talking with MJ by her side, chatting away about the people, the distinct rodeo smells, the stalls, and how she wants to see every single thing. 'I love the whole feeling of this place, the energy. And it's the festival of me, yay!' And she spins off in another direction.

'Who'da thought we'd ever be at a rodeo, eh?' I marvel to Angel, who is laughing with the joy of the moment. 'I mean, this is just so,' I pause, looking for the right word, 'not *us*.'

Angel immediately pulls me into line. 'Speak for yourself. It might not be you, but it *is* CJ. Look how happy she is.'

She's right. CJ is like a starry-eyed kid at a carnival. We're all experiencing the moment together but seeing it differently. I spot a sea of caravans and tents in the distance, and shudder at the thought of camping in any kind of structure. I only want to sleep under five stars, but as soon as I think this, I have to roll my eyes at how bourgeois I am, and how different and privileged my life is compared to Mum's, growing up on the mission in lesser accommodations than these, living on food rations and without electricity.

I think the heat's making me feel a little uneasy and grumpy. All the things going on, the rides, the kids, the food, it's all a bit overwhelming, even for someone like me, who once loved the chaos of the city. CJ is singing out to us because we're lagging behind. She gestures in the direction of a group of women nearby. 'Look, all the women, even the teenage girls, are wearing pearls. I need some pearls.'

Angel and I exchange a glance. We've just found CJ's birthday present.

MJ starts sniffing aggressively and follows her nose to the smoky BBQ food truck.

Angel and I follow CJ into a huge shed with clothing and jewellery stalls, where she stops to look at belts with incredible buckles. Angel links her arm through mine and we set off to find CJ's pearls. Within minutes, we both zoom in on the same pair of earrings, just the right size for CJ's tiny earlobes.

When the pearls are beautifully wrapped and we're back outside, we spot MJ and her smoky BBQ headed towards us. CJ throws one of her booted legs over a bench seat, then the other, dusting off the table with her hands for all of us. MJ's biting into her burger before she's even seated, mumbling while chewing 'OMG. OMG.'

'Good, eh?' I laugh. If anyone enjoys a good feed and drink, it's our MJ.

She takes another bite and savours every chew, catching the sauce dripping down her chin.

'I don't know why they don't do pulled roo,' I say. 'I'd eat that.'

Angel turns away slightly from the sight of all that meat and pulls our gift out of her bag. She starts to sing 'Happy Birthday' to CJ. MJ swallows quickly and we both join in.

'How did you know?' CJ squeals, holding the pearls up to her ears.

'You literally told us!' I laugh. 'And we're glad you did, because we really had no idea what to get you this year! Now you've got the full look of a wannabe rodeo queen looking to ride a cowboy!'

CJ is almost speechless. She gets up and wraps herself over each of our shoulders, kissing our cheeks. 'I LOVE THEM!'

She slips them onto her ears as I look at my watch. 'Okay, CJ, you're slipping. According to your itinerary, it's time to move to the stands and start watching the campdraft.' Right on cue, MJ finishes her burger.

As we walk to the grandstand, I whisper to Angel. 'There aren't many Blackfellas here.'

As she always does, Angel starts to Google then hands me her phone as she digs in her bag for her reading glasses. I start reading aloud.

'"Warwick was founded under its original name of Cannington in 1847. It became Warwick within its first couple of years, and by 1861 was expanding rapidly".' I pause momentarily, and then keep reading. '"And there's seven different Aboriginal language groups around here".'

'Founded, established, discovered, invaded, colonised, settled,' CJ summarises, making notes on her phone.

'Your job in the classroom would be easier if the "grown-ups" elsewhere could use their words better too, don't you think?' I ask her.

'Absolutely,' she replies, holding her own phone up. 'And as there's nothing at all about local mob on the local council website, other than a non-specific Acknowledgement of Country at the bottom of the page, I'll be writing letters to the mayor and the local media this week.'

Angel points to a row of flags beside the grandstand. 'At least they've got our flag flying,' she says. 'Canadian,

American, Aboriginal. Seems like rodeos are international, even here in Warwick.'

As we make it to our seats, I'm observing it all in fascination, the demographics of the people, the way they're dressed, the murmurs of conversations around me. Then I hear something that makes me double-take. 'Did he just say that horse's name is Touch Me There?'

MJ is laughing. 'Yes, and I love it.'

CJ is in her element, beaming from ear to pearly ear, loving all the fashion. 'You can tell the serious rodeo-goers have made an investment in their outfits,' she says. 'So much money on jeans and you know those shirts aren't cheap either.'

I'm scanning all the different outfits. 'I don't get it, though. Where else can you wear this wardrobe?' I look at my own denim skirt, which cost $11 at the op shop. 'I think we might stand out as the city slickers we are, girls.'

MJ shakes her head. 'You spend heaps on your activewear,' she points out. 'We all wear what we need depending on the circumstances. Most of the folks here probably don't buy espadrilles and sandals at the same rate we do, so I'd say the expensive jeans and boots are a solid investment for this crowd.'

I look around the stand through this different lens and start to appreciate how the women have put their outfits together: checked shirts, dark denim, the pearls. Three women in their early 20s sit in front of us and their makeup is immaculate, professional-looking. I know CJ is excited about seeing the rodeo queens and princesses come out later, but right now she's oohing and ahhing over the kids trailing their parents, dressed like little mini-cowboys and girls.

'Don't be getting all clucky, that's not going to get you laid.' MJ nudges CJ, who hits her on the arm and tells her not to be so crass.

Angel springs suddenly to her feet, pointing to some palomino ponies entering the ring, with little kids riding and the mums running alongside. Angel always wanted one as a kid and I can see that little-girl-sparkle in her eye. I can't help but think how hard it must be for the mums running in the sandy ring.

There's so much activity going on around us, people coming and going, dust in the air, beers and Bundaberg rum being passed along the rows. It's a true feast for the senses, and the curator in me is looking at the fashion as an artform, the sea of colours, different shades of blue denim, and the red dust of the ring.

My interest is being challenged, however, by the throbbing that's increasing in my toes, which are completely crushed in the boots MJ loaned me. I couldn't find a pair I liked enough to fork out the dollars for, but I'm starting to regret that. I try to focus on two rodeo clowns in the ring. Their jokes and songs about politicians go down like lead balloons. I want them to stop, because it feels like at any minute things will turn into some Trump-like rally. I can feel the hair on my neck stand on end. I've been warned many times about the everyday racism in south-east Queensland. Thankfully, the clowns are harmless, the crowd chuckle occasionally, then music begins to play over the speakers.

MJ, CJ, and Angel link our arms, swaying left to right and singing 'Sweet Caroline'. Angel, as always, is leading the vocals, and the girls are really getting into it. I look around to see that no-one else is singing or swaying, and nor does anyone else look so much like a bunch of city slickers as we currently do. As if she can read my mind, MJ loudly says, 'Yes, we stick out like dogs' balls,' then keeps singing. I'm always amazed at how comfortable MJ is in her own skin, not giving a damn about what anyone else thinks. Like Angel, who sings at the top of her lungs anywhere, anytime, and unironically wears crocs. There's joy to be had in witnessing that confidence, something I think I lost in Sydney. But I can feel their way of doing life is slowly bringing my old self back.

When the singing ends and the clowning finishes, we're back to spying out cowboy candidates for CJ, not only in the stands but also on the program.

'Aim high,' MJ suggests. 'If you're going riding tonight, you may as well pick the best in the stable.'

My arse is killing me from the metal seat, so I stand up and rub my behind. 'I'm going to find the dyilawa,' I say. 'I bloody well hope it's not a portaloo, cos if it is, I'm driving back to the motel to pee.'

Angel laughs. 'You're so dramatic,' she says. 'Can you please grab me a vegan-beer from the bar on the way back? I'm parched.'

'Look at you, all beer-connoisseur,' I joke. 'I'll be back shortly.' I make my way down the grandstand stairs, through the security check, and follow the other women heading towards demountable-style toilet blocks.

My phone rings on my way to the bar. It's the Murri radio station in Magandjin wanting to yarn about the gallery. The timing's not ideal, but I'm so excited about what's going to unfold in the weeks and months to come, bringing my creative visions to life and helping artists fulfil their own artistic dreams, that I talk to them live for a few minutes, pacing in a near-empty marquee, one finger pressed against my left ear to block out the noise.

When I finally get to the bar area, it takes me more than a minute to work out the ticketing system to buy a drink, and the pickings are slim on the menu. I feel like a crisp, icy-cold sav blanc, but it's only beer or UDL on offer. The cowboy ahead of me is getting his tickets and flirting with the ticket seller, and I'm getting increasingly impatient. My throat is dry from the dust and my toes are now numb from the too-tight boots.

I'm about to reach high to tap the cowboy on the shoulder when he's finally served and turns around. His deep brown eyes meet mine, and I take a step back, breathless, almost losing my balance with shock.

'Ma'am.' He tips his Akubra, and smiles with the best set of teeth I've seen on the showgrounds today. That smile alone could melt all the icecaps in Antarctica.

The face is familiar but the rodeo outfit unlikely, although I think it suits him. 'Daniel?' I ask, confused.

The cowboy laughs so hard he coughs. 'Oh, Sweedard, you've got the wrong brother. I'm Dusty, the good-looking one. And you are?' He waits politely as I struggle to find the words.

'Oh, I'm Annabelle – I – I met Daniel yesterday, in town.'

'And he didn't tell you he had a very good-looking brother?'

I'm flustered. 'No, umm, I mean, he told me his family – your family – were stockmen and women, but he didn't say you were . . .'

'Good looking?' His grin widens.

I have to laugh and can feel myself blushing but hope he can't notice it through my brown skin. He isn't just good looking, he's drop-dead sexy, but I'm sure he doesn't need me to tell him that. 'No, Daniel didn't tell me you were a cowboy.'

Dusty pauses for a moment and looks away, tilting his head as he listens to something in the distance. I wait and notice that he's tapping his foot to the song drifting in from the ring.

His presence is actually mesmerising. My mouth is dry and my palms are sweating. How can he look so much like Daniel but have such a completely different effect on me?

'Miss? Miss?' The woman serving at the bar sings out to me. I drop back to reality and buy a beer, taking a sip immediately to ease my throat and to calm my out-of-control nerves. Dusty's attention has come back to me, a smile still twinkling in his dark eyes.

'I better get back to my friends,' I say, hoping he can't hear nervousness in my voice. 'I'm this way.' I start to walk off but find him loping easily alongside. 'Are you riding today?' I ask after a few seconds.

He nods. 'Sure am.' He offers nothing more.

'What's the name of your horse?' I want to learn more about him, and honestly also half hoping he's feeling something physical, too. *Of course he is*, I tell myself. *He's only human.*

He tells me his horse is Sir Lancelot as he rolls a smoke. I'm vaguely disgusted by the cancer stick, but I'm mainly focussed on the lips he sticks it between.

'That's an interesting choice,' I comment, unsure what makes for a 'normal' name for a rodeo animal. 'Touch Me There' is a far cry from 'Sir Lancelot'.

I watch Dusty's mouth move as he tells me his horse is named after his hero, Lancelot Albert Skuthorpe, who passed away in the 50s, a legend that everyone still talks about. Dusty pauses to lick the cigarette paper and I'm now fixed on his tongue. I'm feeling things I haven't allowed myself to feel since I left Sydney. *Get a grip, woman*, I tell myself, then immediately think, *Hey, I'm only human.* Maybe CJ is onto something with her cowboy fantasy.

'You and Daniel, you look the spitting image of each other,' I marvel out loud. 'But you're so . . .' I pause. I don't want to say that I find Dusty sexy, which never crossed my mind with Daniel. 'You're both so different.'

Dusty chuckles like he knows what I *didn't* say, and I can see this fella is TROUBLE.

'Yeah,' he says. 'Danny-boy is the nice, clean-cut, arty-farty one. He hates all this.' He nods in the direction of the ring. 'He can't stand getting a little red dust on his fancy shoes.'

I thought all Blackfellas loved visual art, dancing, music, storytelling. I must look confused, because Dusty asks, 'What's up, Sweedard?'

'Why? I mean . . .' I wonder how to ask someone a question about their lifestyle without it sounding like a criticism or a judgement. 'I mean, how did you get so involved in rodeos, in this lifestyle, if that's the right word?'

He motions for me to sit down on a nearby bench. The third step I take is into a pile of steaming horse dung.

'Shit! Literally!' I exclaim, loud enough for a little kid nearby to stare at me like she's my mother. I smile at her, then start scraping my boot along the ground in frustration. I look up at Dusty. 'Sorry.'

'No need to apologise to me, Sweedard. Hearing people stepping in horse shit is music to the ears 'round here.' He gently takes my arm and gestures for me to sit on a nearby railing, helping me up. Then he takes my boot off, and cleans it on the grass nearby, no effort, no drama. 'Here you go.' He puts the boot back on, and I try not to wince as my toes are squashed again. *This is turning into a Cinderella rodeo nightmare.*

'You asked me why we're rodeo folk.' Dusty picks the conversation back up, his ciggie perched on his bottom lip. 'Well, I grew up on a cattle station, and my Uncles, all of them were excellent horsemen. They broke in horses.

The best was my Uncle Roy, on my mum's side. He was known as Campdraft Roy. He was, and *I* am, a proud Black cowboy.' He takes a drag on the cigarette.

I'm moved by the pride in his voice as he talks about his history and identity as a Black rider. 'What exactly *is* campdrafting?'

Dusty blows smoke out through his nose and proceeds to tell me that campdrafting is very technical. 'The rider works their beast out there in the "camp", doing a course of sorts. The judges mark the rider on their control of the animal.'

'And you do it as a career because . . .?' I really want to understand why this is his chosen sport.

'Skills, Sweedard. It shows the skills of the rider. Of me!' He winks, and I try not to swoon off the railing.

Dusty's confidence is almost unnerving. I wish I had a better mix of confidence and humility, and I suspect that most of the women I know also suffer from imposter syndrome about the stuff that they're legitimately great at. I wonder if Daniel thinks about his artwork as a demonstration of *his* skill, married with his passion for his politics and for the environment.

'So, all the men in your family do this? I mean, except Daniel?' I ask.

He laughs, and then I'm surprised to hear that most of the women in their family ride, too. 'Naomi, my sister, was five years old when she started. The women in my family do *everything*,' Dusty says proudly. 'I grew up watching them drive cattle. They fenced, cooked, they were involved with everything. If there's anywhere women have true equality, it's right here.' He nods again to the ring. 'We had that women's lib stuff long before the city folk.'

'City folk?' I don't even know why I'm protesting the term. He takes my hand without a word and inspects the perfect shellac manicure, so I don't say anything more on the subject. 'How old were *you* when you first rode?' I ask.

"Bout four or five years old? When I got my first horse, Trigger. All the kids had horses, even Danny Boy. Daniel only ever groomed his horse, though, and drew pictures of it.' Dusty laughs, which makes me feel uncomfortable, like he's having a joke at Daniel's expense, and I'm supposed to join in. I focus instead on the twinkle in Dusty's eye.

'Did you travel around to rodeos?' I like the sound of Dusty's voice, too. It's throaty, no doubt from the smoking. I watch him look around the grounds as he rattles off places around Central Queensland: Alpha, Jericho, Emerald, Rockhampton, Ballandean. He tells me the rodeo circuit is an exciting life and a real family event for him, and for most riders.

I raise my eyebrows in surprise and Dusty keeps talking. 'Kids watch the older people. They're role models, even in the dangerous events like bronco riding. They learn the skills very young and then end up here.' He gestures to some other cowboys walking by.

As the crowd cheers in the background, I feel like I've gained a better understanding of rodeo life in our brief exchange. I want to share it with Angel, who hates any event that uses animals for sport or entertainment.

Dusty tells me he's got to go, calls me Sweedard again, and asks for my number. It's the least romantic pickup I've ever had, but I can't get my phone out of my bag fast enough. There's at least a dozen texts and three missed calls from the girls as I add Dusty's number.

'Shit! I've got to go, too.' I offer a handshake, but he just winks, tips his hat, and walks off.

I weave through the crowd as quick as I can to find the girls waiting with a mix of concern and suspicion. I'm hoping I don't smell like horse dung.

'You took your time,' Angel says.

'Where the hell were you?' MJ is grumpy. She tells me I missed out on some great selfies. Angel is looking at me expectantly. Her beer!

'Oh shit, I drank your beer, Angel! I'm so sorry. I think I just met the hottest cowboy here, and I guess he made me thirsty.' Then I see CJ's face full of anticipation. Double shit! 'Sorry, CJ, I was trying to get a handle on this world, how kids grow up to be on the rodeo circuit.' I stop at telling her I gave Dusty *my* number and not hers. Triple shit. I soldier on before she can ask. 'You will NOT believe who he's related to. He's the brother of Daniel Davies, the artist we met yesterday.'

'No way! There are *two* hotties?' MJ exclaims.

'Yes! And get this, they're literally like chalk and cheese. His name's Dusty. He's on the program, his horse's name is Sir Lancelot.'

'You'll have to introduce me.' CJ is on the edge of her seat. I know that's why we're all here, but honestly, I want him all for myself.

'He's riding in the third round,' I say. I should admit to the girls I fancy the cowboy, even though I have zero in common with him, but something is stopping me. I know wanting him is ridiculous and not wanting CJ to have him is even *more* ridiculous. My teenage self has come flooding back and I vow to find CJ someone else.

The opening bars of the national anthem pipe in over the speakers and MJ looks wordlessly at us. None of us ever sing it. Everyone gets to their feet as a young local girl, probably getting the biggest break of her singing career, sings her lungs out. The four of us stand up slowly because we know to pick our battles and don't want to draw attention to ourselves by remaining seated.

'Let's just support this girl's singing career today,' I whisper to my cousin. We all stand awkwardly in silent protest. As the music continues, my mind wanders back to the bar and the electricity I felt between Dusty and me. A wave of heat begins to rise through my chest as people start sitting down.

CJ taps me on the leg, mumbling about learning to score the riders, but I'm not really listening. She and MJ talk about the lack of clapping for competitors, and they get all caught up in their own conversation. Meanwhile, Angel is chatting to the people sitting behind us.

And then I hear the loudspeaker and my heart skips a beat.

'Next up is Dusty Davies on Sir Lancelot! Dusty's gonna stick to that beast like chewing gum to a shoe!'

We all watch intently as Dusty rides Sir Lancelot with determination and skill, driving the cattle around the course to a roaring cheer from the crowd when he finishes.

'He's incredible. I can't wait to meet him!' CJ nudges me, but before I can say anything, we're all giggling as the MC announces the next rider on Touch Me More. We decide to come up with some horse names ourselves.

'I'd call mine "I Touch Myself",' MJ announces with a wink. We crack up again, as do the couple sitting behind us, who by now know all our names. When the four of us are together, our sense of fun and frivolity is infectious.

\* \* \*

Later that night, as the popular country band starts their gig and we're getting crushed among all the locals and travellers, I find myself checking my phone constantly, hoping Dusty will be in touch before we leave the showgrounds. Finally, just after 9 pm, there's a message:

Where are you, Sweetheart? I'm in the bar near the northern grandstand. Come over.

'Anyone want a drink?' I sing out over the Wolf Brothers, holding up my empty. The other women hold up their cans and give a 'no thanks'. I'm relieved. As I weave my way through the crowd, my heart is thumping in my chest and I can't feel my feet at all anymore. I reach the bar and see him, surrounded by checked-shirted, pearl-eared, boot-scooting, gorgeous women. I feel deflated. They all look so comfortable, like they belong here, they fit in here, they have things in common with Dusty the Cowboy. Things I don't have.

'Sweedard,' he sings out over the crowd, and I look behind me in case there's another *Sweedard* he's calling to. There doesn't appear to be, so I smile and walk towards him, still feeling nervous and inadequate. I start some self-talk: I'm a strong, deadly woman, and I am all I need to be, for me, for *anyone*.

'This is Annabelle,' he announces to the group, who all smile and greet me warmly. I'm surprised at how hospitable and friendly people are at the rodeo. But then again, why wouldn't they be?

Within minutes, Dusty has a beer in my hand and his own hand on my left butt cheek. *He moves fast*, I think to myself, a little taken aback but a little glad at the same time. It's been months since a man has touched *any* of my cheeks. I put my reaction to Dusty today down to the fact that I need a bit of action. He leans down to whisper in my ear. 'You're the prettiest gal here, Sweedard.' I *know* that's not true, but I'm doing all right and his words make me smile.

I swear I haven't had more than three sips of my beer before Dusty is guiding me through the bar, through the back security checkpoint, past the marketplace to the sea of campervans I'd spotted that morning. We don't speak on the way and I don't care.

Inside his van, which is an impressive modern set-up, he gently pulls me to him, one hand on my butt, the other behind my head. He kisses me softly at first, then his tongue is searching, we're glued to each other, and I want his tongue to search some more. I peel his black shirt off.

\* \* \*

I wake early the next morning and immediately remember the way Dusty's hands felt on my skin, his breath hot on my neck, and his tongue between my thighs. Then another thought intrudes and I'm abruptly horrified.

'CJ!' I bolt upright in bed. 'Oh no!' During the drive back to the motel last night, the car was completely silent and CJ was so upset. They all were, once they realised I'd slept with Dusty. They'd looked for me all over the showground, texting, calling, speaking to security, only to find me walking towards them over an hour later, dishevelled and grinning stupidly.

MJ was unusually mad at me and asked what was going through my thick skull. I thought that was a bit rough. I'm not an idiot, I was just horny. Angel spoke to me like a disappointed parent, ready to call the police. CJ said she was worried, but I know her words hid her disappointment in me, too. I felt even worse when I learned that CJ had been dancing with someone promising but had to leave them because she went looking for me.

I sit in bed and hate myself for a few more minutes, vowing to sing all the country songs, wear whatever I have to wear, buy everyone the biggest lunch possible. Then my mind drifts inevitably back to Dusty. I start trawling the internet to learn as much as I can about him, about his career and Sir Lancelot. Mostly, I'm searching for photos of him with women. A man that hot and that smooth would have to have women *everywhere*.

I find mentions of Dusty Davies on professional rodeo sites and learn that his role model 'Lance' was a showman and a storyteller, a master of bush ballads who wrote his own PR material. I scan every horsey-looking Insta page I can find, click on hashtags for his name, but whenever he appears, it's just him and his horse. I'm grateful and disappointed at the same time. There *must* be women, *somewhere*.

I put the phone down and put the kettle on. As I tip a sachet of Nescafé into a mug, my phone pings with a text, and I nearly break my toe on the corner of the bed racing to read it. *Please be Dusty.*

It's Angel:

Morning! We're meant to head out at 10 am! It's in the itinerary. Are you still good to go? Or got OTHER plans?

I ignore Angel's crack and hope that everything is back to normal when we leave.

Hey there. Yes, good to go at 10 am, will be at the car just before to load it up.

As the others pile into the car, CJ sits in the front passenger seat and starts reading the itinerary for the day. First stop is the cheese factory, then a cellar door, followed by the Big Apple and the apple shop, Ugg boots and bakery to follow.

'Are we good?' I ask quietly. 'I mean, I hope you all know I'm really, really sorry I made you worry last night, and that I went AWOL without telling you. I know that's not how we do things. I don't know what came over me.'

'But you know *who* came over you, don't you?' MJ laughs.

I'd normally join her laughter, but I'm completely serious right now, because it's CJ I'm really worried about. 'Are you and I okay, CJ? I didn't mean to rain on your sleep-with-a-cowboy parade.'

CJ pats my hand. 'I know, but I'm going to play on your guilt for a while because I know you well enough to know you *will* have guilt.'

'I'll give you the money for the Buckeroo Hotel you lost, too,' I offer.

CJ tells me not to worry, that's she got a credit and might come back another time and try again. I don't know what else to do or say, and I'm almost grateful for the grilling the girls start giving me about Dusty and our interlude, because it means they're no longer angry with me. When I finish my semi-censored version of events with Dusty, I test the waters about seeing him again, but the responses aren't what I want to hear.

'Why would you? You can't *date* a cowboy, you're *you!*' Bullets of common sense come at me, fast and furious.

The fact that Dusty smokes and calls me 'Sweedard' are at the top of the list. I laugh when CJ says that. As a teacher, she could've given him a health lesson and an elocution lesson all in one night.

When I suggest with a wink that CJ would also want more than one night with him, she punches me in the arm, pretending to be angry for having all *her* birthday fun.

My head agrees in principle that I shouldn't see Dusty again, but my loins are in strict opposition. What harm could it do to have some fun with someone I won't have to run from?

# CHAPTER FIVE

The April mornings are starting to cool down, humidity has finally dropped, and it's a later start to running with the shorter days. I've been running regularly with Michael for a month now and I really enjoy his company. He's quick-witted and makes me laugh a lot about silly things, like the way Blackfellas say 'aks' instead of 'ask', and 'pacific' instead of 'specific', and the way we can spot other Murris out running by their skinny ankles. Today I take a second to admire the newly trimmed beard and mo he's sporting, making his smile somehow brighter and his eyes a deeper brown under his mop of mocha hair. I may need to remind MJ about his good looks – I don't think she ever ended up making that move she was so keen on.

'New look?' I ask as he stretches against the front fence of our property, his calves smoothly muscled.

'Yeah, picked it up on special last night in the city.'

I chuckle and hit him in the arm. 'Wow, are they new too?' I joke about his bulging biceps, then blush and wished I hadn't. I still don't want him to think I'm flirting with him.

He cracks some joke about finding them in the bargain bin.

'Okay, smart-arse, let's go,' I say. 'I think 5 k and back by 7 am is a good goal.'

Michael is off and running before I can even set my watch to start and I have to work hard to catch up. We run and talk, or more accurately, we run and *I* talk. As has become our usual routine, Michael seems to ask all the questions, appearing genuinely interested in my work. As always, I love talking about the gallery. It's hard to imagine a Blackfella who doesn't appreciate art. Dusty flickers across my mind and I remember Daniel saying his brother doesn't value his work.

Since the rodeo, Dusty regularly texts and calls, but we rarely talk about my work. Dusty usually starts by asking me what I'm wearing. On the other hand, Michael is interested in the arts, fitness, and life in general, a rare find. Maybe it will take two men to give me everything I need.

As we reach the 5 km mark, my phone pings, just as my watch clicks over to 6.59 am. 'Woo-hoo! That's a good start!' I high-five Michael and quickly glance at my phone. It's Dusty and seeing his name makes me smile.

We walk into our front yard and Michael tells me he's going to the races on Saturday with a group from work. He invites me to join them.

'That sounds like fun,' I begin cautiously, then pause, trying to find the words. I'd love to get frocked up and have a day out, but I've taken a stand for a few years on not supporting horse racing. CJ, Angel, and MJ all feel the same, especially about the Melbourne Cup in November. We get dressed up the day *after* the Cup instead and go out without feeling guilty. I feel weird about it now, though, because the RSPCA has similar criticisms about rodeos and bull riding. It feels hypocritical to be interested in Dusty when that's his life.

I don't realise how long it's taking to process all these contradictions until Michael nudges me to check I'm not having some kind of episode. 'Sorry, was I frowning? I do that a lot when I'm thinking.'

Michael laughs as he stretches his hamstrings. 'You were looking a little ferocious, yes.'

'The thing is, I'd really love a day out, but I don't support horse racing.'

To my surprise, Michael puts his hand up immediately. 'Say no more, I understand. I've been looking for an out myself. You've inspired me to tell them the truth, like you've just done.'

I'm relieved he doesn't think I'm a party pooper, though I know I haven't been *completely* honest with him. But it's time to go. 'Thanks for the run. See you tomorrow for 6 in 36?'

'You're on. Let's head to the markets on Saturday instead of the races? No need to frock up for that, unless you want to. I need to stock up on my fruit and veg.'

'Yes, yes, yes! Great idea,' I say as I head into our building. I race to get inside my flat and to Dusty's text. He's opened with his standard morning greeting but today there's also an invitation.

> Sweetheart! Missing me? Want to meet me in Beaudesert for the campdraft? Not a lot of red dust there, but plenty of black love for you.

I go weak thinking about the kind of Black love he offers. I've played our rodeo romp over and over in my mind every single day for the last three weeks. Maybe it's completely illogical, but I think I miss him. Or maybe I miss the sex. Either way, I've lost control over the longing. I haven't told the girls, though, for fear they won't understand something I barely understand myself. Today, with a meeting with Daniel only hours away, I'm riddled with confusion *and* desire. I text back, noncommittal.

> Black Love sounds fun.

I'll need to google campdrafting later, but right now I need to get ready for a meeting with the other Davies brother.

At 10 am, Daniel walks into the gallery, with a swagger different to Dusty's, but nevertheless a swagger. It must be genetic. He's already met the staff and most of the committee, and everyone loves him, his energy, his style, and most importantly, his artwork. I know he'll be a huge hit for the gallery and for Murri artists. I've always believed that when one does well, we all do well. This is the work I enjoy most, the excitement of making my vision come true.

'We need to confirm the number of pieces we can have in the show,' I tell him. 'And you need to decide *exactly* which ones you're happy to hang, because it's a selling exhibition and I know you've earmarked pieces you want to donate to different charities.' I've been really impressed by his ethics, generosity, and the way he gives through his craft. 'Did you still want to run that workshop with the kids from the community centre? Because we can create a workshop space upstairs easily.'

Daniel is enthusiastic. 'Absolutely, can't wait, Annie. Squeeze in as many kids as you can. I love working with young people.'

I continue to ignore being called Annie and make a note to get the workshops coordinated. Daniel stands to leave, so I stand and walk him out of my office and into the gallery shop. His phone rings and my phone pings simultaneously, and we both nod a farewell to each other before I head back to my desk. It's Dusty again. I'm surprised by the level of his attention today.

Miss me, Sweetheart?

I reply:

Do YOU miss ME?

Ten seconds later:

Of course, I do. You're my little bull rider.

What follows is a string of seductive messages that make me blush. I'm confused and horny and I know I can't keep it from the girls any longer. I want their advice, even though I'm probably going to ignore their wisdom if it's not what I *really* want to hear. I text the group chat.

Have a confession to make and need some advice. Anyone free for bevvies at The Boundary after work?

Over the next couple of hours, I laugh at all the messages in our Whatsapp group as each of my tiddas try to guess what my confession might be. I don't say anything, waiting to see them later.

When I arrive, they're all waiting, drinks in hand, food on the way.

'What the hell is it?' MJ asks as soon as I sit down.

'There's something I haven't told you,' I say nervously, holding my phone.

Angel puts her hand on top of mine, looking concerned.

'I'm not sick,' I quickly add.

MJ takes a long sip of her wine, one eyebrow raised.

'Whatever it is,' CJ says sincerely, 'you know we'll always have your back, Annabelle, always.'

I breathe in and out, long, and deep. 'Since we got back

from CJ's birthday weekend, I've regularly been in touch with . . . Dusty.'

'What? How? Why?' There's so much racket with the questions that I'm confused as to who's saying what. At some point, Angel mutters, 'Jesus wept', MJ sculls her wine, and I wish I hadn't said anything at all. But it's too late, the cat – or rather, the cowboy – is out of the bag.

'He contacted me a few days after we got back, and then it just turned into every morning texting and some late-night calls and . . .' I trail off.

MJ wants me to give all the dirty details of our sexting, but I nip that in the bud.

'I am *not* going into details with you, MJ! I think we need to turn the romance spotlight on you at some stage. Are you still unhinged on Hinge or just tipsy on Tinder these days? Do tell!'

'Whatever it takes to get some attention,' MJ huffs and takes another gulp of wine. 'My beautician is the only person whose seen my vag in months. That painful Brazilian wax needs a bigger audience.' We all crack up but Angel pulls us back to the topic.

She suggests that Dusty is probably texting a few women, and that doesn't impress me at all. 'Thanks, cuz.' I can't blame her, but I do tell them that I couldn't find anything online about him, no photos with women.

'So, you and Dusty, eh?' MJ asks. 'The man who calls you *Sweedard*?'

'Just so you know, that's only the way he says it. It's his accent, that's all. He spells it properly.' I'm feeling protective of Dusty, which I know is a sign that I like him. 'Here, this is my morning greeting!'

They all look at my phone, and MJ laughs so hard wine comes out her nose. I pass her a tissue and shake my head in mock disgust.

Angel puts her hand on mine again, but firmly this time, less an act of concern and more one of big-cousin-seriousness. She says sternly, 'He's a professional cowboy, Annabelle. He rides and ropes cattle, which you said you disagree with, *and* he smokes!'

'Yes, yes, yes!' I put my head in my hands for a few seconds. 'And there's more.'

The three look at me with similar expressions. 'What more could there possibly be?' CJ asks.

I take a breath and blurt the rest out. 'He wants me to meet him for a campdraft thing down the coast.'

MJ is the first to have a crack. 'Oh, this is gold! You didn't even want to go to CJ's rodeo birthday, but now you're thinking about following a bloke to the Gold Coast – a cowboy, a smoker, *and* probably a guy who has a woman in every grandstand? I mean, you could at *least* go for the brother. He has some taste and he's arty, and I'm sure you could get him to stop calling you Annie if you wanted him to.'

Angel and CJ nod in agreement and I feel like I'm under attack. 'Wow. Why don't you all tell me what you *really* think? I mean, you're being a bit harsh, aren't you? This is why I haven't mentioned anything to you until now. What happened to our non-judgemental coven?'

They look somewhat chastised, but none respond. I can feel an angry betrayal bubbling inside me. 'We didn't judge *you* when you wanted to fuck a cowboy for your birthday, CJ. We all got on board, and we supported you and your fantasy.' I can't control my tongue now. 'And you, Angel, no-one judged you when you went home with Kev the first time you met him at some hippie party, while he *still* had a girlfriend. And we were happy for you when you fell in love. AND we don't say anything when you mention him 100 times a day. We know he loves you; we know he brings you a cup of tea every morning; we know how much you do everything together, but you know what? Your single friends don't need to hear about how great your relationship is *all* the time. And yet, we *are* still happy for you. And you, MJ, this is so rich coming from you when you keep your love life between you and those apps. But we don't judge you and we *always* make sure you get home safely. Because that's what sistas do. Support and understanding without judgement.'

A painful silence follows, and I know the others feel as crappy as I do.

'So, thanks for the support tonight. I *really* appreciate it. I know he's not The One. I know he's different. But I thought you'd appreciate that while I'm married to my job right now, sometimes I get lonely, and I want to feel beautiful and desirable, even for a short while, even if it means I must make some compromises. And maybe he's okay for me right now.' I stand up. 'I've had a long day, and this,' I wave my hand across the table, 'this just made it feel even longer. I'll see you all later.'

Angel grabs my hand and says softly, 'We're just watching out for you, that's all.'

I look at Angel, MJ, and CJ and I see sadness in their eyes. 'I know you are, and I knew you would say all the things you said, but I . . .' I swallow the emotion rising within me, 'I just really want to see him. And it would mean the world to me if the women I love the most just said one positive word to support me.' I race out of the pub as tears begin to form.

Before I've reached home, my phone is going crazy with messages from the others, apologising and offering boots, blinged jeans, and other items to make their friend fit into the campdraft scene. I'm still feeling raw, so I don't respond and head to bed instead.

I can't think of anything I'd rather do less than go running in the morning. I text Michael:

Hey there, sorry to do this so late, but I don't think I can run tomorrow.

He responds immediately:

Are you okay?

I can't tell him that my friends probably think I'm emotionally crippled *and* desperate.

Just a bit flat.

I put my phone down and turn out the lamp, but I'm surprised when my phone pings again.

> Okay, then let's just walk, easy pace, grab a coffee. Endorphins and caffeine. The best way to start the day.

I know Michael is right.

> You are a very smart man. Thanks. I'll see you at 7 am. Good night.

Just as I go to turn my phone off, it pings.

> Sleep well. Tomorrow is a new day.

\* \* \*

I'm surprised when Michael hugs me when we meet in the morning. It's just what I need, and I fall easily and appreciatively into the warmth and strength of his arms. I can't remember the last time I was hugged so firmly.

'How did you know I needed that?' I ask.

He smiles his toothy white smile. 'I have a sixth sense,' he jokes. 'And sisters. Did you sleep well?'

'Actually, I was so tired, I just crashed.'

We start walking south at an easy pace, as he'd promised, and he asks if I want to talk about whatever is on my mind.

As a bush turkey crosses the path in front of us, we stop, wait, then keep moving. It gives me time to consider if Michael will understand the issue I'm facing. Surely he's dated people that weren't right for him. Everyone our age has at some point.

'My friends think I'm naïve.'

'I find that hard to believe.'

'Believe it,' I insist.

He laughs a little. 'Going out on a limb here, but *are* you naïve?'

On a normal day, I'd have laughed too, but today I stop abruptly, chin quivering.

He bumps my wrist gently, prompting back along the path. 'Hey, I was just kidding,' he says softly. 'You're one of the smartest women I know, and I know quite a few smart women.'

I don't know if Michael will judge me too, but I need a male perspective. 'There's this guy,' I begin.

He nods. 'Of course there is.'

I stop again. 'What does that mean?' I ask defensively.

He takes me by both arms and looks me straight in the eye. 'It means you're a gorgeous, intelligent woman, so of *course* there's going to be a guy somewhere. But if you keep stopping, we won't get very far on our walk this morning.'

I nod and start walking again. 'He's someone who my friends think – and I deep down *know* – is completely wrong for me. But . . . I like him, even though there's zero logic to my feelings . . .' I shrug.

'The heart has its reasons which reason knows nothing,' Michael says. I look confused and he explains. 'It's something Blaise Pascal said. The heart is the centre of your emotions and feelings, but it's not your mind, which is for thought and reasoning.'

I haven't got the brain to think about French philosophy right now, so I tell Michael about Dusty, that he happens to be the brother of the spotlight artist for my gallery opening, that he lives outside Magandjin, that he smokes, that I didn't think I could kiss a smoker, that he calls me Sweedard. Michael can't see any deal-breakers there, though he reckons he couldn't kiss a smoker either. He asks if Dusty is as career-driven as me, because *that* might be a deal-breaker. I feel like there's a positive here.

'Oh, he's career-driven! *Very* competitive in his field.' And then I have to work the truth a bit when Michael asks what Dusty actually does. 'He works with animals,' I say vaguely.

Michael takes that to mean that Dusty's a vet, which is an admirable vocation and a difficult degree to complete. Oh, how easy it would be if Dusty were a vet.

I take a deep breath. 'He's a cowboy.'

Michael laughs.

'What's so funny?'

He's still laughing when he asks, 'A cowboy? On a horse? With a big hat, and chaps? Ropes cattle and stuff?'

I close my eyes and nod. 'Yep, that'll do as a definition.'

We go back and forth about how I met him at the rodeo, how he's the brother of an artist I'm working with, how the girls haven't met him but already don't like him, how we all know he's probably not going to turn out to be the great love of my life. Michael asks me if I'm actually looking for my great love and I have to think for more than a few seconds.

'I wasn't looking for *anything*. It just happened. We met. There was something there.' I don't think Michael needs the full kiss and tell. 'We've kept in touch ever since, and now he wants me to meet him down on the Gold Coast for a campdraft.'

Michael wants to know what a campdraft is.

I laugh. 'To be honest I still haven't got a clue.' I jump on Google as we walk. 'Good old Wikipedia says that campdrafting is a unique Australian sport involving a horse and rider working cattle. The riding style is Australian stock, somewhat akin to American Western riding and the event is like the American stock horse events such as cutting, working cow horse, team penning, and ranch sorting.'

Michael naturally reminds me that I didn't want to go to the races with him, and that I boycott Melbourne Cup as a stand against cruelty to animals. 'But you're planning on going to a *campdraft*, which is probably as much fun for the animals as horse racing is?'

I'm embarrassed on so many levels. 'I know! I'm a hypocrite. That's part of the dilemma! You think I'm naïve too, or even a bit loopy, don't you?'

Michael shakes his head. 'For starters, no-one says "loopy", and secondly, I think only good things about you, but this doesn't make sense to me. Even for the non-reasoning, Pascal heart. Is Dusty at least a decent guy to make the ethical compromise worth it?'

I give a small smile. 'I think so. I'm working with his brother and he's a great guy. I assume Dusty is decent too. But I guess I shouldn't assume anything.' As we turn into our street, I remind myself that Daniel and Dusty are like chalk and cheese. Why should I assume anything about Dusty being like Daniel?

\*\*\*

When I catch up with the girls later in the week, I tell them about my yarn with Michael. 'You'll all be pleased to know that when I asked Michael for his advice about Dusty, he said, and I quote, "I'm probably going to err on the side of whatever your girlfriends think you should do, because they know you and what's best for you." I thought you'd appreciate that.'

I smile to let them know I've moved past our last conversation. I know how much love there is between us, how much we care about each other, but nevertheless, MJ apologises on behalf of the three of them.

CJ sits with hand on heart. 'I've felt terrible about how we acted all week, Annabelle.'

'You know we love you and will support you in whatever choice you make,' Angel adds, blowing me a kiss.

'Oh, I know, we all support each other,' I quickly reply. 'And I know sometimes we have to be brutally honest in that support. I'm sorry for being so harsh, too!' I'm relieved because I don't like conflict with my tiddas. Life is too short, and work provides enough stress without drama in my friendship circle. 'Thanks so much, ladies. I don't want to argue over a literal roll in the hay.' I quietly hope there's something more civilised than Dusty's horsey-smelling van on the coast.

'So what have you decided to do?' Angel asks. 'You're going to meet Dusty again?'

I take a deep breath and nod. 'I know it's just a fling, but maybe that's what I need right now. I've said so many times that I'm not looking for a relationship at the moment and I meant it.'

MJ nods wisely. 'Ah, Charles needs a break, I get what you're saying,' she jokes.

That comment is met with groans and giggles, and I'm glad we're back to normal.

'I was hoping I could borrow your boots again, MJ?' I ask.

She raises her glass in agreement, but is clearly surprised. 'I thought they crushed your toes?'

'Clearly, I'm a sucker for punishment,' I admit. 'Thankfully, after his event, we're going to have a couple of nights at Broadbeach and the Groundwater Festival is on at the same time. I'm pretty sure I can wear my normal clothes there.'

Angel googles the festival program and reads out the highlights, and CJ promises to give me some tips. She went to the festival last year to see Troy Cassar-Daley play, and casually mentions (as she always does) how she went to school with his wife, Laurel, a legend on the mic in her own right. She also offers to make me a bespoke itinerary.

'I think this is better as a go-with-the-flow trip,' I say. 'I think being on the beach, listening to some music, away from the animals and dust, it might be a good opportunity to see Dusty out of *his* comfort zone, and get to know each other better.'

CJ and Angel smile, but I know they're not convinced. MJ is distracted and frowning at her phone, so I ask what's wrong.

She looks up. 'I've got a baby shower to photograph this weekend. The mother just texted to say the number of guests have doubled. I'm going to need some help.'

'I'm free,' I immediately volunteer. I don't really know what the day involves, but look forward to being on the job with MJ at one of her gigs.

'That'd be great, thank you. I honestly don't even know why people still throw baby showers.'

'I've always thought those parties are more about the parents,' CJ replies. 'A kind of like, let's celebrate we made something together, before it even arrives.' There's no sarcasm in CJ's voice, but with none of us being parents ourselves, there's a lot we don't understand about the motherly frame of mind.

As we step out onto Boundary Street, I wait till the others are well and truly out of sight before I go into an op shop and buy myself a pair of dark denim jeans with bling on the butt that fit me perfectly. I tell myself I can pick the bling off later, keep the jeans and no-one will be the wiser.

\*\*\*

It's a stunning Magandjin morning as Michael and I head over the Go Between Bridge and make our way to the markets in West End. The crowds are already building in search of the best fruit and veg, but we first join the queue for coffee at the famous Caravan. Caffeine in hand, I have to use every ounce of willpower to restrain myself from ordering gozleme or a breakfast kebab, but I do grab an almond croissant to have later at home.

Michael grabs my hand because I'm dawdling and steers me through the locals armed with envirobags and shopping lists. We stop at what he insists are the best tomatoes he has ever eaten.

'Look at these,' he says, holding up the ripest, reddest of the fruit there is.

'Marambangbilang!' I exclaim and startle him by seizing the tomato from his hand, taking a good long sniff, then biting right into it. 'This is so good, deadly!'

He loads his basket up, promising to make me his special pasta sauce, and I grab some for salads in the coming week.

'Oh. My. God.' I take off towards a fresh seafood and meat van. 'I think they have roo today.' I listen to the young fella spruiking all on offer, and when he pauses to take a breath, I interrupt his script.

'What roo do you have?' I ask, excited because it's the only red meat I eat these days and it's been a little while since I had a good serve.

He rattles off mince, snags, steaks, roasts. I want them all but have a small freezer. I opt for two kilos of mince, a tray of snags, and suggest a couple of steaks for Michael to BBQ, but he turns up his nose at the suggestion.

'Oh, I don't think I could eat Skippy,' he says, shaking his head.

'But you can eat Wilbur?' I ask pointedly as he orders some pork chops.

'I don't know what you're talking about,' he replies with a smile, tapping his credit card with one hand and taking the chops with the other.

'Um, *Charlotte's Web*?' I feign outrage.

He outright laughs at that. 'Tell you what, if you spot a message in a spiderweb about eating roo, I'll consider it.'

I follow him through the crowd, making a mental note to cook him something sometime when he's not thinking about eating the national emblem.

We grab some bread and flowers, throw some gold coins into a busker's guitar case, and make our way back to Michael's car. It's not even 8 am and I feel like we've achieved quite a bit. It's amazing how good company can jumpstart my day.

Back home, I'm smelling of bleach and doing boring domestic chores, wishing for some more of that good company. I text Dusty about our planned rendezvous.

> Can you send me the deets of where we're staying for the campdraft pls? Here's the place on the GC. Can't wait to have an ocean swim.

I send the link to the high-rise hotel and Dusty replies with the name of a caravan park. I search it online and look through the interiors of the cabins and vans. I'm a bit worried I'll be claustrophobic sharing close quarters with Dusty, but don't bring it up. Instead, I text him:

> And I've got a surprise for you, I'm sure you'll like it.

He fires a reply back immediately:

> As long as it involves you naked, I know I'll like it, Sweetheart.

Dusty's texts always make me smile and blush at the same time, but it's time to meet MJ for her baby shower gig, and I regretfully sign off and promise to message him later.

MJ is waiting on the street with her gear when I pull up. We load it all into my car and head out to the event. When we arrive, there are cars lining both sides of the suburban street, with multi-coloured balloons tied to the letterbox and cheers coming from the back garden.

'Are we late?' I ask MJ, who shakes her head as she walks to the back path.

'No, we're right on time. I think they've probably started early.'

In the backyard, there are long tables with gorgeous cakes, sandwiches, and other finger foods on offer. A bar has been set up for adults and a fairy floss machine for the kids. The family have gone all out for this baby shower.

'Wonder what the 1st birthday will be like?' I mumble to MJ, who grins as she checks the lighting, fiddling with two different lenses. I'm in awe of MJ's talent and the range of photography she does, from parties like this to family portraits, weddings, people's pets, she's across it all. I know these kinds of events are just about making the cash to pay the bills so she can do the more artistic and political protest photography that mean so much to her. I'm glad she needed help today, just so I could see her in action again. In the future, I'd like to have MJ's work exhibited at GoFNA. I'd have asked her to be part of the opening actually, but the memory of the perceived conflict of interest in Sydney is just too fresh. Even though everyone knows everyone in the arts scene, the fact that MJ and I are *so* close may raise some questions in some minds. I just need to get a couple of exhibitions up before I can give MJ that kind of platform, but I'm confident she'll shine when I do.

She hands me a gold reflector to carry. 'I thought these were usually silver?' I ask.

'Gold reflectors are better for outdoors because the gold catches and amplifies the hue of the sun,' she explains, then walks around the party taking candid shots of the family and guests as they arrive.

I have a lightbulb moment. I may not feel able to do an exhibition with MJ just yet, but I can *certainly* hire her for the opening. There's so few professional Murri photographers locally, and flying someone in would be prohibitively expensive. MJ makes perfect sense and I almost squeal.

'Tidda, we need a local photographer for opening night. Can you do it? Please?'

She doesn't look up from the shot she's lining up, but I can hear the smile in her voice. 'I thought you'd never ask.' I laugh and she continues. 'I've got some great ideas already and I've made some notes about a social media strategy as well that we should talk over. But right now, we need to capture the kids in action.'

After some party games, the presents have been opened, the huge vanilla cream cake has been cut and distributed, the party thins out, and MJ's work is done.

Looking at how happy the couple are, I can't help imagining what it might be like to be so excited about bringing a new life into the world. Sometimes I think opening night of an exhibition is a bit like birthing something, without the stretchmarks. It can be the same amount of time to pull off something significant in the arts, sometimes even longer. And for those of us who aren't remotely maternal and have chosen our careers over motherhood, those artistic achievements are like our babies.

# CHAPTER SIX

The traffic is flowing smoothly along the motorway as I leave Magandjin the following Friday morning. I've had little sleep, tossing, turning, trying to think about what I'll say when I first see Dusty, and what I'll say after that. We've only had short bursts of conversation on the phone, and it's not exactly been small talk. That's something I left out of the confession to the girls – the dirty talk, or the 'Dusty talk' as I've come to call it. I've been thinking that Dusty must have a type – a rodeo queen type – so I'm not even sure why he's even interested in me besides my body. And, of course, the off-the-charts-hot sex.

To distract myself from that line of thinking, I run through what I packed for the one day of the campdraft and the two days on the Goldie: two pairs of jeans (one with a blinged butt), MJ's boots and thin socks, eight tops, denim shorts, denim skirt, two linen dresses, sandals, and my running gear. I've got Troy Cassar-Daley blaring through the car, and I've added some other country singers I heard at the rodeo to my playlist, trying to get in the mood. A wave of nausea washes over me and I know it's nervous anxiety. I usually only get this feeling on opening night or when I meet with funding bodies. Today, though, I'm excited like a kid on a school excursion, but I'm also scared. What if we see each other and the chemistry isn't there anymore? What if the electricity I felt when he touched my hand at the rodeo has dissipated? What if I'm just on the motorway to embarrassment and humiliation?

As I near the showground, I drive by the site slowly, like Nanna Sony use to do when she wanted to see who was on the bowling green before she decided to go in. There are tractors clearing the earth in the ring. It's just on 10 am and I want to see what the women are wearing before I go to the caravan park to change. From what I can see, it's like the rodeo, but less dressy, and there are no pearls in sight.

I get into my cabin not long after. I booked my own at the girls' suggestion, in case things go pear-shaped with Dusty today. I'm taking things one day at a time – if all goes well, then the Gold Coast will be wonderful. If not . . . well, then at least I can lick my wounds on the Goldie.

Within minutes, my clothes are strewn throughout the cabin as I try on every piece of clothing I brought with me. I decide on the blinged dark jeans. They feel unexpectedly comfortable, but I convince myself that's because my high-waisted skinny jeans are just too tight.

When I arrive back at the showground, I sit nervously in my car for 15 minutes before I head through the turnstiles. I make a beeline straight to the food and clothing stalls. When I was at the rodeo, I'd taken very little notice at all. I feel a pang of guilt at not having shown more enthusiasm back then, especially for CJ, my most trusted tidda.

'Good morning, Miss,' a friendly gentleman says, welcoming me into a hat stall. 'Can I help you?'

'Oh, I'm just looking, but thank you.' I have my hand on a hat and quickly remove it.

'I think this Maverick would look perfect on you. May I?' When I smile and nod, he gently places it on my head.

'There,' he says, stepping back to look. 'Hey, Bill, bring the mirror over here,' he sings out to his colleague who is manning the register.

'Perfect, George, perfect.' Bill holds the mirror up to me. 'If you wear that to the bar tonight, well, you'll surely find yourself a husband, Miss.'

'Might find yourself more than one husband,' George suggests with a wink, and I giggle.

'You fellas should sell cars, you're so good at this. But I need something that doesn't really look like I'm at a rodeo?' I don't want to offend, but when I see the price of the hats, I know I need one I can also wear in the city to get my money's worth. 'I need one I can wear back home, too.'

The two men nod and get busy finding the right hat just for me. By the time I leave the stall, I've bought the perfect Maverick after trying on 10 styles. I also walk out with a cowgirl-ish top in my favourite purple (after also trying on 10 different styles), and I thank Bill and George, who aren't fazed at all by the effort it takes to please me. 'I know I'm probably the highest maintenance customer you'll have today,' I tell them, 'but I want you to know that I actually feel gorgeous in this. So, thank you!' They wave me off, assuring me that I look fantastic.

As I walk out into the sunshine, I wonder if Dusty will find me even more attractive in my new gear. I snap a selfie, sending it to the girls and adding it to my own Insta stories. I feel less self-conscious, less obvious as a city slicker.

Over the loudspeaker, the MC announces the start of the day. 'Welcome to the Melbourne Cup of Campdrafts,' he says excitedly into the microphone, unfortunately reminding me of my conversation with Michael about my contradictory ethics. I push that thought to the back of my mind. I'm here now and all that matters is seeing Dusty.

I still haven't texted him to let him know I've arrived – I wanted to feel comfortable in the space before I did that. I'm still not 100 percent sure I'll even stay, with my confidence and self-esteem ebbing and flowing. I climb the metal stairs to the grandstand, find a seat, and start to look for Dusty. I can't see him in the pen where the riders and the beasts are released from, so I focus on the action when the next rider enters the ring.

Rider after rider does their thing, and I try to understand the scoring. From the commentary and the conversations around me, I think that riders and their horses can earn up to a total of 100 points. A 'cut out' is worth a total of 26 points, horse-work is up to a further 70 points; and four points for the course, and they have 40 seconds to complete the course and go around the pegs. It slowly starts to make sense.

'That was an incredible attempt to earn 100 points by MK Hall on Mr Nice Guy!' I listen with interest to the MC announcing scores, now that I know a little more about what I'm watching. 'That's 73 in total for horse-work, coursework, and contact.'

After a break, the program shifts and I enjoy watching the Ladies Barrell Race and the Ladies Breakaway Roping that follows. The MC rattles off horse names like Duck Yeah, Murri Prince and Black Knight, so I assume there's some other mob competing, too.

And then his name is called.

'Dusty Davies on Sir Lancelot –' and then everything is just white noise as all my senses are channelled into the sight of Dusty, my proud Black cowboy, centre stage. I'm mesmerised by his movement in the saddle. I immediately want to feel him naked, and shift in the seat. And then he's gone. Scores are given and the moment has passed. I wait a few moments, then text him.

> That was amazing. You're amazing. I'm in the grandstand, where should I meet you?

My arse is numb from the metal, the legacy of having a flat Koori butt with not enough flesh to pad the bones.

Once again, I can't feel my toes in MJ's boots and I swear to never wear them again. No man is worth it, not even Dusty. My phone pings, distracting me from the aches and pains.

> Sweetheart, I need to be here a while longer, why don't you take your pretty self back to the caravan park and I'll meet you there.

*Thank God!* I think to myself, but respond a little less enthusiastically.

> Good idea. See you soon.

I take my boots off in the car, and when the suds in the shower hit the raw skin on my feet shortly after, I'm cringing. My back aches from the hours on the stadium benches and I don't feel sexy at all. I check my phone before I dress and there are messages from the girls, Michael, work, and Aunty Elaine, who wants to yarn about my cousin graduating back home. The last is the only one I respond to, as Aunt is at the top of the respect hierarchy.

There's a knock at the cabin door. 'You in there, Sweedard?'

'Uh, yes,' I call through the closed door. 'I'm just out of the shower.'

'Music to my ears. Why don't you drop the towel and let me in?'

I don't move. 'I've got to make a couple of calls. I'll pop

by yours in a few minutes, okay?' I'm glad I got my own room just to have a little of my own space and some privacy. I've always lived alone as an adult, run my own race romantically, had my own plan for life. Men have only ever been a side dish to the main meal. And I've never completely been in love, not like Angel and Kev are. So while I'm excited about seeing Dusty, I'm also aware of my own needs and realities.

He seems unbothered. 'Okay, I'll grab us some beers.' I hear his boots tromp off.

*The romance of it all!* I wryly think to myself. Then again, beer is probably befitting my bruised bum and blistered feet.

A few minutes later, I try not to limp as I head barefoot to Dusty's cabin, where he's sitting on the verandah with his feet up and shirt off. His brown, ripped torso makes me thirsty and hungry at the same time. 'Doesn't take much for you to get your shirt off, does it?' I laugh, putting a basket of nibbles on the table and then taking a seat in the other chair.

'No reason to hide the goods, Sweedard,' he drawls with a smirk. 'Why are you limping?'

I know my first in-person conversation with him since the rodeo shouldn't be complaints but I can't help myself. 'The boots I had on today, I borrowed them from MJ. They literally crushed my toes and I have blisters. See?' I lift my foot.

He takes that foot and lifts the other into his hands, inspects the boot damage, then leans in and tenderly kisses each toe one at a time, little pecks that melt my heart and make me squirm with desire.

'Stop!' I half-protest, enjoying the moment but conscious that there are kids playing in a family cabin across the way. I do a little wave in their direction. Dusty nods decisively, then swoops me up, throws me over his shoulder and carries me into the cabin, where I squeal as he playfully tosses me onto the bed.

Then he *really* kisses my feet, his tongue between each toe, driving me crazy. I pull my t-shirt and bra off, his mouth moving up my legs while I undo my skirt. He lifts his head and grins while he watches me aggressively tug my skirt and knickers down with a quick yank. His grin widens when I place my hand on the nape of his neck, suggesting he get back to my legs.

As the night unfolds, my bodily woes take an orgasmic turn for the better, and when Dusty leaves the sex-rumpled sheets for a cigarette, I just stretch out, yawn, and drift off to sleep. I'm woken to the sound of a twist-top beer bottle being opened a short while later. Dusty is at the small table in his boxers, TV on but turned down.

'Sorry, I nodded off.'

'Sorry I woke you,' he returns. 'But a man's not a camel.'

'There's some cheese and bread in the basket, on the verandah, if it hasn't gone missing.'

He ducks out and returns with it.

'You should eat something. *I* should eat something.' I wrap the sheet around me, suddenly famished, and fix us both something to eat with our beers. I sit at the table. 'It's a bit of a squeeze,' I say, feeling cramped.

'Nah, Sweedard, it's cosy!' He drops a swift kiss on my lips and I giggle like a schoolgirl.

'Were you happy with today?' I ask, unsure what would please a competitor other than a win.

'Yeah, I had good rounds and I'm happy with my numbers.'

'Why do you do it?' I ask, biting into the bread as if I haven't eaten for days. 'Is the win the Holy Grail, or is there more to it?'

'Damn straight!' he says. 'It pays well and offers more money than any other campdraft in Australia. And I'm good at it.' He sips his beer. Asking how much the pot is worth feels rude, so I resolve to google it later. But he must know what I'm thinking, because he laughs and says, 'Sweedard, I don't get out of bed for less than $10,000.'

I'm surprised by the number and how good he really must be. *At least I didn't fall for a mediocre cowboy*, I think drily to myself. 'Are you the Evangelista of cowboys then?' I joke but he just looks blank. 'Google her,' I laugh.

He tells me that campdrafting is one of the fastest growing sports in Australia. When I can't hide the mix of surprise and suspicion on my face, he grins cheekily. 'Google it.'

\* \* \*

The smell of the sea air fills my nostrils not long after we leave the caravan park and I'm grateful the campdraft is over. We check into our high-rise and I'm psyched for the next two days at Broadbeach.

Dusty takes a firm grip of my hand. At first I think it's a romantic gesture, but when he almost breaks my fingers, I pull back. 'What's wrong?'

'I'm not good with heights,' he says, moving to the back of the elevator, leaning against the mirrored wall.

'We're on the 34th floor,' I tell him. 'Is that going to be a problem? If so, I'll ask for another room on a lower floor.' I want him to be happy, but I love being as high as I can be. He doesn't answer, so I fill the silence. 'I actually wanted this room because of the view. You'll understand when you see it. I had a weekend here last year with the girls, and it was amazing.'

When the doors open, Dusty drags both our cases as I lead the way to room 3404.

'It's only three days away, what've you packed in here?' he asks.

'Your bag is the same size!' I counter as I open the door and let Dusty pass with the luggage. 'Ta-da!'

On the white countertop is wine, chocolates, and other amenities, courtesy of the manager. It's standard when you're a platinum guest, but I play it down because I don't think Dusty is likely to be impressed with the number of five-star hotel stays I've had.

I head over to the balcony. 'Do you want to try and have a look at the view?' I ask gently, just in case.

Dusty walks slowly to stand next to me, stopping before the glass doors. He looks out to the sea, then glances slightly downwards and says, 'Whoa!' He steps back, one hand on his stomach. 'That's a long way down.'

'Do you get vertigo?' I ask, stepping back with him, taking hold of his hand.

He doesn't answer and I feel bad. I need to explain. 'Dusty,' I take both his hands now and he grips mine briefly. 'I wanted to make it a surprise, but the Groundwater Country Music Festival is on this weekend. So I was thinking we get the best of both worlds – the ocean for me and country music for you. And this gorgeous view. Win, win.'

'Win, win,' Dusty repeats, dropping my hands and stepping further back into the room. He points towards the horizon. 'Those clouds suggest we might get some rain, unless that wind keeps up, then they'll continue moving south. But right now, it's a scorcher, so I'm gonna jump in the shower, Sweedard.'

I sense he doesn't really want to go into whatever his issue is with heights, so I let the matter drop. I'll just have to keep an eye on him and see if he starts to look uncomfortable or ill. 'Sure, I'll unpack and organise some cool drinks.'

He disappears into the bathroom, and as I start sorting through my bag, I can't wipe the smile off my face. I feel happy, content, more comfortable in the familiar surrounds of city life, modern hotels, and the ocean breeze. The seaside is one of the few things I miss since leaving

Sydney and my favourite hangout at Maroubra beach. There's a spring in my step as I put my clothes away and change into cut-off shorts, a sleeveless white linen top that I tie in front and my Maverick hat. I've even got glittery runners for the festival. Funnily enough, I want to be a little country at Groundwater and can't wait to check out the stalls set up next to the surf club.

There's no way I could've shared that cabin with Dusty – we would have been falling over each other constantly – but this sizeable apartment is perfect for our time on the coast. I feel like I'm playing house as I organise the place. *Now* this *is my kind of cosy*, I think to myself.

My phone pings with a text from Michael, but before I can look at it, Dusty reappears, a towel slung low on his hips, beads of water on his chest and torso. I nearly melt into a puddle of lust.

'Well, helloooo, cowboy!' I saunter over, undoing the buttons I'd done up only minutes before. Within seconds, I'm standing in front of him, naked but for my Maverick hat. He pulls me close and we stumble to the bedroom.

'Well, I hadn't done that before,' Dusty drawls later, lying back with one arm behind his head, the other around me.

'Done what?' I ask. I thought they'd been some standard moves on both parts.

'Had a doori in a high-rise apartment,' he explains.

I can't help but chuckle.

'What's so funny?' he asks, sounding a little defensive. 'You know, not everyone lives the big city life, Sweedard, and some of us don't want to either. Just because I choose a small country caravan park over a city high-rise doesn't mean I'm somehow not as good or as smart as you. In my world, I'm the best at what I do. I just don't flaunt my success.'

My cheeks burn at his words, remembering my hesitation when I first saw the caravan park online. Does he think I flaunt my success, my privilege? I'm sure this room suggests I do. I gather my thoughts.

'I wasn't laughing at you.' I don't think I'm fibbing. 'I was laughing because I haven't heard the word doori for ages.' That *is* the truth. I get out of bed and get dressed, hoping that it's not going to be awkward between us now.

'Am I too country for you, Sweedard?' he asks, watching my every move. I feel like he's angling for an argument by pointing out the differences he perceives between us, and making me sound like a bourgeois Black *and* a bitch at the same time. But then, maybe I *have* given off vibes suggesting that I think he's a country bumpkin, and then I see myself as he sees me, and I hate myself. I think quickly on my bare feet.

'Not at all.' I walk to the balcony and call back inside, changing the subject. 'Let's go check out the stalls and some of the acts. The music sounds great.'

Dusty doesn't answer. I wait a couple of minutes, and when the silence becomes too much, I go back inside, to find him sound asleep, looking like king of the castle in the huge bed. I kiss him on the mouth and for a fleeting moment consider crawling back into bed with him, but

I pull away because I really want to be in the sun. I leave a note on the table.

*I've gone for a walk to the festival. Rest up. Text me if you want to meet up. XO*

Within minutes, I am weaving through the stalls, loving being able to take my time looking at vinyl records. I've only ever seen a collection like this at my aunt's house in Wagga Wagga. I stop at a stall selling beachwear and I find a pair of boardies with the Murri flag on it. They're way too big for Dusty, but they have a pair of budgie smugglers that will fit him perfectly and show off his hotter-than-hot body. I buy them, hoping he'll wear them to the beach with the same confidence that has him swaggering everywhere else. Further on, I see people throwing something in the cornhole arena, but stop to watch punters try out the Hot Tomato Bucking Bull. I wonder what Dusty would think of it as entertainment, as a copy of the real thing. The ticket seller tries to encourage me to have a go, but I pretend I'm not interested. Deep down, though, I think that if Dusty were here and he thought it was a good idea, I'd give it a go.

The sun is hot and I'm grateful for the ocean breeze as crowds start to spill into Kurrawa Park. There are a few stages with bands and soloists performing for free, and I sit for a while to enjoy the acts on the main stage.

My mind wanders back to the room, but I've never been one to stay indoors when there's an alternative, not even for a hot cowboy. Maybe that's why I'm single. But *am* I single? I don't know what Dusty and I are. Are we dating? Are we exclusive? Do we need to talk properly about it, or not?

\* \* \*

The sun is setting on Saturday, and I'm enjoying the view from the apartment after the festival. A chilled sav blanc is in my hand, and when Dusty finishes getting dressed, I push a chair closer to the sliding doors and away from the balcony's edge. 'Here,' I say. 'If you focus on the horizon, maybe the height won't bother you so much?' Although Dusty isn't comfortable out here, he sits and rests one hand on my thigh, the other wrapped around a beer. 'I love dusk on the coast,' I say happily. 'With so much happening at the festival, it's busy and exciting, yet peaceful at the same time.' I sip my wine then look at Dusty, who is just smiling at me. 'What?' I ask suspiciously.

'You're gorgeous,' he replies. My heartbeat quickens, and heat rises up my chest and neck. 'I love your hair and your smile. I love the way you smell. I love the sound of your voice and how soft your skin is.' He runs his hand up and down my thigh.

'Well, that's four of the five senses covered,' I joke.

He leans in and whispers, 'I love the way you taste, too.'

Within seconds, we are back inside and naked, and I am working on all his senses as best I can.

When we finally leave the hotel in the afterglow of lovemaking, I am proud to hold my cowboy's hand.

We fit in with the other country music fans and Akubras in the street.

'I sussed the venue out earlier today. We head this way.' I lead Dusty through the crowds who appear to also be heading to Troy Cassar-Daley's show on the Back Road Theatre stage. When we arrive, rows of white chairs are lined up and a couple of women in fringed boots are dancing and having a ball. 'This zone is booze free. We'll have to sit up there if you want a beer,' I say, walking towards some empty seats.

'I'll grab us some drinks,' he offers. 'What do you want, Sweedard?'

'Surprise me.'

I watch him head to the bar with his natural, swoon-worthy swagger and I grab two seats to the left and front of the stage. I'm less inclined to swoon when Dusty returns and offers me a choice between a UDL or a can of Bundy and Coke. I choose the vodka and there's something about sharing it with him that makes it feel almost natural. He taps his can to mine. I'm not keen on putting my mouth to the can – God knows how many hands have touched it before mine – but I wipe the rim with a tissue and take a sip. Dusty's eyes follow my movements, but he doesn't say anything.

When Troy Cassar-Daley comes onstage, the crowd erupts in applause and Dusty whistles so loudly people metres away look over at us. I can't tell if they're annoyed or impressed, but Dusty doesn't notice, just taps his foot to the tunes being belted out, one hand resting on my thigh the whole time. Troy encourages the audience to sing along to 'Dream Out Loud', and many take to their feet, including Dusty and me. We're both singing the chorus, but I notice that Dusty knows the words to the entire song.

He hums all the way back to the hotel as we walk with our arms around each other's waists. When we reach the lift, he positions himself against the mirrored wall at the back again. Not even the booze has relaxed his nerves. Though I know I'll have a hangover in the morning, I'm glad the third UDL has left me a bit tipsy – and horny.

'You know what we should do right now, Dusty?' I ask with a cheeky grin as we get back into our room.

Dusty responds by kicking off his boots and unbuckling his jeans the minute the door is closed behind him.

'Hang on!' He looks confused and disappointed when I hold up a hand. 'I think,' I continue in a sultry voice I hardly recognise, 'that we should fill that big bath with bubbles, grab a beer, and slide in there together.'

Without a word, Dusty heads to the fridge, grabs two beers, and walks to the bathroom. One of the things I'm really appreciating about him is that, for the most part, he's easy-going, far less complicated than some of the visual artists I've worked with, whose creative minds are always switched on and over-analysing everything. Dusty's simplicity is refreshing in so many ways.

As I lay in the bath between his legs, my back resting against his chest, Dusty caresses my breasts and hums to himself.

'What's that tune?' I ask. 'I'm sure I know it.'

'It's my dedication to your beautiful boobs, Sweedard.' Then he starts to sing in a gorgeous, rich baritone and I recognise the tune at last.

I nearly pee myself. 'Oh my god, "Islands in the Stream"?' I gasp. 'That is *hilarious*. And you have a beautiful voice.'

'Sing it with me, babe,' he urges, singing louder, and I realise he's more pissed than I am.

'I can't sing, unless it's Koori-oke or Murri-oke and there's a lot of background noise to drown me out,' I joke, taking another sip of beer.

Dusty keeps singing both Kenny and Dolly's lines and he's so easy to listen to. I've long been interested in Dolly Parton's politics, so I mention it. 'You know Dolly Parton turned down two Presidential Medals of Freedom? One from Donald Trump and one from Joe Biden. I always thought that was interesting.'

Dusty drops back to humming the song, still playing with my breasts.

'And she had a lot of power in uniting Americans during the Trump administration, too,' I continue when he doesn't say anything, 'when his vile politics were tearing the country apart. I read that her concerts brought the most unlikely audiences together, from both sides of the political spectrum. That's a good thing, don't you think?'

He doesn't say anything until I nudge his thigh with mine. 'If you say so, Sweedard, I don't really do politics.'

'She's a big supporter of literacy, too.'

'I'm not a big reader,' he says, running his tongue along the nape of my neck and manoeuvring his hand between my legs.

\* \* \*

Not committed to meeting Michael for a run or walk, I sleep in on Sunday. The sun is high and streaming into our room when I finally strain to open my eyes. We really need to pull the curtains of a night. I look at Dusty as he sleeps. He looks so peaceful, without a care in the world. I wonder if he's dreaming about me. I want to touch the cute dimple in his chin. I'm jealous of how flawless his skin is, surprising given the smoking and the amount of Coke he drinks. There are only a few lines around his eyes, too, despite a life in the outdoors. I push some hair off his forehead and accidentally wake him.

'Morning, Sweedard.' His voice is raspy with sleep and sends a shiver through me. 'Come here.' He pulls me into him, his naked body warm against mine.

'Babe, I need to go for a run. It's already hot out there.' I sit up.

'It's hot in here, too,' he mumbles, pulling the sheet away from my body, and I know we're seconds from another session in the sheets if I don't get a grip.

'Come with me!' I invite him as I slip from the bed. 'It'll do you good, burn off some of that booze and beef from last night.'

He's not having a bar of it. 'I'm the fittest man you'll ever meet,' he tells me as he watches me put my running gear on.

'Really?' I scoff.

He rattles off his workout regime most days: jumping jacks, lunges, burpees, planks. 'I've got what you women call core strength,' he says with a wink.

I can see the ripple of his six pack from the corner of my eye, remembering running my hands and lips over it many times in the last 48 hours. 'I think everyone calls it core strength, not just "us women",' I reply, trying to stay focussed.

He sits up, the sheet barely covering his lap, and it's so tempting to just strip off and climb back over him. 'What I do out on Sir Lancelot is as tough and dangerous as rugby league, but it also requires the finesse of a figure skater.'

'You're sexy when you use fancy words like finesse, say it again,' I smile.

'And I've got the strongest groin in the land.' He throws the sheet off and stretches his naked body out. It's the most glorious thing I've seen in the male form ever. He waves me over and whispers, 'Come here, my little bull rider. Don't fight it. Come ride the strongest groin in the land.'

I *am* only human and I can't resist. I tell myself it's okay not to run today, that I burned enough calories and worked enough muscles last night to count as a workout.

When we've both finally worked out enough, I'm ready to get outside. 'Let's go to the beach and have a dip before it gets too crazy.'

Dusty is not as keen. 'The beach isn't really my thing, Sweedard.'

I'm disappointed. 'But I bought you something special,' I say, rummaging through the drawers and pulling out a plastic bag. I hand it to him with enthusiastic pride.

'I don't need gifts,' he says, 'but thanks.' He opens the bag and his tone changes. 'What the . . .' He pulls out the budgie smugglers with the Murri flag on the bum. I'm sure he thinks they're undies.

'For the beach,' I explain.

'I'm not wearing these, to the beach or anywhere,' he responds firmly, holding them up to the light. 'Should we even have the flag on our butts?'

Fair question, but I'm disappointed again. I don't want to make a big deal of it, and I'm sure Dusty will not appreciate my being a sook. He can read my face though; he pulls me close to him and explains.

'You're very generous, Sweedard, but I don't wear these dick sticker things. I hardly ever even swim. The last time was in the Condamine River when I was a teenager. I don't even own a pair of shorts. Have you *seen* my wardrobe, Sweedard?'

I'm willing to acknowledge that it may not have been as thoughtful as it could have been. 'But you can't wear denim and dark shirts to the beach.'

I think I've hit a nerve when he tosses the swimwear to the chair near the bed. 'I can wear whatever I want,' he says dismissively. 'You're never going to make me into a surfer dude.'

'I'm not *trying* to make you into a surfer dude,' I say defensively. 'I wore checks and blinged jeans for you. I crushed my feet into boots for you.'

'When did I ask you to do any of that?' Dusty asks, exasperated. 'You would've looked beautiful in a potato sack.'

I can feel tears threatening. 'I was trying to fit in, show I was interested in what you do, your lifestyle.'

Dusty leans back, his hands behind his head, completely calm, and it unnerves me. 'You don't have to do any of that for me.'

I don't want to fight and don't want to feel like shit. 'I'm going to the beach. I'll be back in a little while.'

I will not let a beautiful day on the coast be ruined, and by the time the lift reaches the ground floor, I'm close to being re-centred. When I cross the road, the market stalls are setting up for the final day of the music festival and families are arriving for their day at the beach.

Positioning myself just left of the red and yellow flags, I rub 50+ into my skin and sit watching the nippers start their events nearby. I'm more focussed on the supervising dads than the kids. Many of them look fit, and they clearly love the ocean. I wonder how many of them are single, how many have their little nipper for the weekends. Not being remotely maternal, I've never really thought about kids myself. But right now, I find myself thinking about what kind of a dad Dusty would be. Certainly not a nipper-Dad, not when I can't even get him to the beach.

A whistle blows and the kids are off and running. Watching them makes me tired, especially after a late night with broken sleep. I lie back, position my sunhat over my eyes, and doze.

'Sweedard? Sweedard.' I think I'm dreaming until Dusty touches me lightly on the arm and I spring upright.

'How long have you been here?' I ask, fixing my sunhat.

'Just a minute. You were snoring.' He chuckles.

'I don't snore.'

He laughs again, then stands up. He's wearing his hat, jeans, a navy t-shirt, and thongs. *At least he didn't wear his boots*, I think to myself. When he takes his tee off, the sight of his lats and the obvious strength in his back takes my breath away. But when he drops his jeans to reveal the cozzies, I want to cry.

'Dusty!' I exclaim. He spins around and his smile mirrors mine.

'I like it when you smile, Sweedard.' My heart melts with the softness in his voice, and he bends down to give me a peck. 'I don't like it when you look upset with me. You don't have a poker face when it comes to disappointment, that's for sure.'

'I'm sorry.'

'Sweedard, if you can wear boots that give you blisters, then I think I can wear these for a minute, though there's not much room,' he squirms a bit, adjusting his balls, which makes me snicker.

He turns around and looks out to the horizon, and I wonder if he's aware of the bikini-clad women nearby, raising their sunglasses and smiling at him.

'Ladies,' he drawls, and throws them a wave. He's seen them all right, and he's loving it.

'Don't encourage them,' I scold, amused and a little jealous.

'Harmless fun, Sweedard, harmless fun,' he says, tipping his hat to another group perving on him as they stroll past.

I have to laugh. 'Sit down,' I say, pulling him next to me. 'Everyone knows you're here now!'

'As long as *you* know I'm here, Sweedard.'

\*\*\*

'I'm a bit sad to say goodbye,' I confess before I can stop myself. *Don't be needy, don't be the first one to say stuff like that*, I rebuke myself. *This is just a fling. You don't have time for a relationship. You need to focus on your work, and you are too city for this cowboy. It'll never work out.* I know these rules – I wrote them. But the words are out and I can't take them back. The silence that follows feels like it lasts for days. Only seconds later, however, Dusty responds.

'I don't want to say goodbye either, Sweedard.' He plants his luscious lips on mine for a few seconds and I'm dizzy with desire. 'We had a good time, didn't we?' He bumps his hip into mine, making me laugh.

'We did,' I whisper in his ear.

'Meet me in Rocky, in a few weeks' time. My nephew is riding, the whole family are going to watch.' He says it fast and confident, and I'm taken by surprise, but respond equally swiftly and confidently.

'Love to!' And I kiss him again, holding it long enough to ask myself if meeting his family means something. I pull back, noticing he has the dreamy look I'm sure I also wear, and decide to ask straight out. 'Dusty, are we exclusive? I mean, are you seeing anyone else?'

'Just you, Sweedard. You're more than enough for one cowboy.'

My heart explodes with joy. I'm not just a one night stand, I'm his *only* stand. I'm not sure how we got to this place so quickly from not wanting anything serious at the start, but as I drive back up the motorway to Paddington, I'm bursting with something more than simple infatuation.

During the one-hour trip home, Siri and I answer all the texts that have been left hanging since Friday morning. I leave MJ, CJ, and Angel till last.

> I need to talk to you. Can you come over to mine next Friday? Drinks and debrief? XX

I turn off the phone and turn on Troy Cassar-Daley, who reminds me that it's okay to dream out loud.

# CHAPTER SEVEN

'Thanks for coming over. I need to debrief, and then re-brief, if that's a word.' I pour a glass of wine for each of my tiddas as they sit around the kitchen table.

Their questions come thick and fast. 'How was your weekend?' 'Are you in love?' 'What's so urgent?'

I sit down, take a breath. 'The weekend was amazing. I'm *not* in love. The urgent matter is, well, Dusty asked me to meet him at another event in a few weeks' time, some bull rider's thing.'

Angel pulls a face. I know she couldn't think of anything worse, and not having a poker face seems to run in the family.

CJ gives me her firm teacher's tone. 'I don't think it would be in your best interest to go.'

'Oh, darl, are you still dirty that Annabelle got the cowboy?' MJ chuckles. It's awkwardly silent for a second, then we all burst out laughing. MJ waves her hands in my direction, urging me to go on.

'We got on well on the weekend, we sang, soaked in a bath, he even wore the Murri budgie smugglers I bought him, and that was a *big* deal, let me tell you. Generally the only time he wants out of his jeans is to get naked.' I smile at that thought. 'He was really attentive, and the *sex*, my god, worth all the "Sweedards" in the world for the sex alone.'

CJ throws her arms up in the air in a comical 'Why not me?' gesture and I'm grateful she's such a good sport. Now that I'm apparently addicted to it, I'm not sure that I'd be quite so forgiving at missing out on cowboy sex.

'Why do you need our advice if everything went so well?' Angel asks. She's clearly googling something on her phone.

'Because his family will be there, too. His nephew is riding and apparently they're *all* going. I'm guessing Daniel will be there, too. I'll need to tell him beforehand.' I pause, wondering how that conversation will unfold. 'It's serious business meeting the family and I don't even know if we *are* that serious. But I wonder what his mob is like.'

'Yep, just as I thought,' my cousin declares. She hands her phone to MJ, who starts reading out loud.

'The RSPCA views bull riding as it does rodeos generally.' She scrolls the screen, mumbling to herself, then reads from their website, '"In December 2017, a bull suffered a broken leg and had to be euthanised during an event in South Australia".'

Angel raises her eyebrows at me, waiting for a response.

'Don't look at me like that! You know I don't support animal cruelty,' I protest.

'Don't go, then. Are you willing to trade your ethics just for sex?'

'Hang on, cuz.' I pause, take a deep breath, and continue. 'The thing is, to my surprise, it's not just sex. We might not have a lot in common, but we really connected, you know? And then we had a bit of a talk and we're exclusive.' I take another deep breath for my next confession. 'I miss him and I want to see him. It's another weekend away together, it could be romantic. You've all been at me for ages about my love life, and my life for months has been working, just work. But now, this thing with Dusty . . . I haven't felt like this for a long time. It feels good. You've been with Kev so long, you seem to have forgotten what it's like to be alone.'

There's silence as Angel contemplates the reality that's just been spoken. My reality.

'Also, Dusty sent me these expensive boots. They arrived by courier today,' I chuckle as I hold them up for the women to see. 'It's not quite Cinderella, but he went and bought boots for me.'

MJ takes the wind right out of my romantic sails, suggesting Dusty would have a sponsor provide these. I screw my face up and flick her the finger.

'Anyway, I like them. They may not be Louboutin, but they are Lou-BOOT-in.' The girls laugh at the terrible pun, and thank God it's become less serious in the room.

I can tell Angel is holding back her judgement as she tries to calculate how long Dusty and I have known each other. CJ, the eternal romantic, just wants to know if I am in love.

MJ shoves CJ out of her seat aggressively before I can reply. 'Move, this requires an intervention.'

I'm annoyed. 'What the hell are you doing?'

MJ points to a spot near the outdoor lounge setting. 'Put your chair there. And you and you,' she points to CJ then Angel, 'we'll place our chairs around her, like a circle.'

'Stop it!' I stand up. 'I don't need an intervention. I need some sensible words from one of you, and clearly that's not you, MJ!' There's tension but I know it will settle, it always does.

Angel walks over, puts her arm around my waist, and eases me back into my chair. She sits next to me and warmly says, 'My dear cousin, you know anything we say comes from our *knowing* you, *understanding* you, and *caring* about you. And . . .' she pauses.

'And what?' I bark.

'I think we all thought Dusty was just some fun, someone to keep you company, but not someone you were serious about, nor in love with.'

MJ pipes in. 'You spend more time with Michael than you do with Dusty, and your neighbour would be a far better match given your city and your healthy lifestyle.'

I can't stop myself from snapping at her. '*You* need to stop talking, at least for a minute, can you do that?' MJ just rolls her eyes and I'm getting a bit angry. 'For the last time, Michael and I are just friends, and we will stay that way *because* we are neighbours. Don't dip your pen in the office ink and all that, right?'

MJ, clearly frustrated, gets up to walk away from the table. 'I don't get you. You're choosing a cowboy over something potentially real with your neighbour because of bullshit pens and ink and whatever? You need your head read.' She slips out to the bathroom. I open my mouth to call her back, but she's disappeared before I have the chance to think of anything articulate.

'What do *you* think, about Dusty?' I ask CJ, knowing she'll be honest.

Her answer is honest, but gentle. 'You don't really have that much in common with Dusty, do you?'

I know it's a more than fair question. 'Neither did my Nanna Sony and the German, and they were in love forever and lived happily ever after, till he died of lung cancer.' I hope CJ doesn't point out that Dusty smokes. 'So it might work?' I don't sound convinced myself, and glance over at MJ, who's returned to the table and is sitting quietly, pretending to look at her phone. When she looks up, I snark, 'Anything else *you* want to add?' Sarcasm does not suit me, but I can't help myself.

'Can I just make one suggestion?' Angel asks, heading off another row.

I nod.

'Before you pack *anything*, just be positive that it's what you want and what *he* wants, too.'

I nod again.

MJ leans over and pours herself more wine. 'I say this with love. Be *absolutely*, fucking *sure* that it's what you both want, *Sweedard*. Because a weekend away, meeting his family, is a big deal, for anyone.'

CJ shakes her head at MJ's language. 'Whatever happens, you know we'll always be here for you.'

MJ starts laughing. 'We'll stick pins in voodoo dolls, if necessary.' She jumps up suddenly and points to me. 'You want me to be more supportive?' she asks.

'That would be nice,' I say.

'Then I'll go to Rocky with you, as your support person!' She walks around the table as if talking to herself. 'I want to photograph some public artwork there. Apparently there're bull sculptures scattered throughout the town. They'll be great to build my tourism portfolio.'

'Aaaaand?' CJ prompts.

'Aaaaand, I can get un-*Hinged* up there for sure. Cattle isn't the only *meat* in Rocky, you know.' MJ picks up her glass and raises it in the air to cringes and bursts of laughter.

The next thing I know, CJ is coming too, in case Daniel is there and needs company, or things go pear-shaped with Dusty's family. Although my tiddas say they're supporting me, it does feel like they don't really have the greatest confidence in me and Dusty.

'If it goes to shit with Rusty, good for us to be around for moral support,' MJ agrees.

'It will not go to shit,' I half-protest. 'And you know his name is Dusty.'

Angel has been quiet this whole time, and it's clear now that she's super disappointed in the three of us, as if we're planning on riding the bulls ourselves. CJ needs Angel's approval, because she hates to be at odds with any of us.

'Angel, I'm only going to keep MJ and her camera out of Annabelle's way. I won't be anywhere near the bull riding,' she promises.

'And the only riding I'm interested in is steamy, consensual riding with two-legged bulls,' MJ adds with a wink. 'Nobody dies at *my* events, but they may feel like they've gone to heaven.'

She links CJ's arm through hers and faces me in a stand-off, waiting for me to cave. And of course, I do.

I look at Angel, shoulders slumped. I know her well enough to know she feels defeated. I pull her to her feet, give her a hug, and whisper seriously, 'I'm not making excuses, but it's a one-off as far as I'm concerned, to see Dusty, to see if there's something more there. But I don't want to go without your support. Please tell me it's okay to go.'

Angel looks at me, tears welling. She's genuinely upset and my heart hurts. 'I just don't understand how you are putting a man before your ethics.'

'Angel, you know I'm against animal cruelty, but you also know I can't argue against something I don't fully understand. These are mob involved, I want to know how and why.'

I'm glad my cousin has asked the question and made me think about what the hell I am doing going to a bull riding event. But her questions aren't enough to stop me seeing Dusty again and she knows it.

She pulls me in for a hug. 'Okay, I just hope it's worth it.'

\* \* \*

The days and weeks ahead are busy, with the August gallery opening nudging closer, and my spreadsheet of tasks getting longer and longer. Daniel and I are in regular contact with phone, Zoom and in-person meetings. At no time during these chats, though, do I feel I can mention Dusty or the pending trip to Rocky, where he is more than likely going to see me. I know I'm going to have to say something eventually, but the time just never feels right.

Then, without expecting to, I bump into Daniel at the First Nations Knowledge Centre that sits within Magandjin's cultural precinct. We're both there for the launch of the local Southeast QLD First Nations Artists Network, hosted by the local First Nations Chamber of Commerce. There are some efforts being made to assist artists in developing their business knowledge and capacity, as individuals and as a collective.

When I walk in just prior to the start of the launch, I spot Daniel straight away. He's got a trendy, young art student hanging off his arm and every word he says. He and Dusty may be worlds apart in their work, but they seem the same when it comes to charming the ladies. I wonder if Dusty is charming another woman tonight, or worse. A pang of jealousy strikes, and I turn to face the river, hoping Maiwar will keep me rational. *Don't assume the worst just because you can*, I tell myself and take a deep breath. It doesn't stop me pulling out my phone to send a text:

> Your little bull rider is missing you!

I'm startled by Daniel's voice behind me and fumble to put my phone away. 'You wear the Magpie Goose label well,' he says, complimenting my outfit.

'Hello to you too!' I turn and smile. 'And thanks, I'm a huge fan of this grassroots enterprise. You should buy your girlfriend a dress.' I nod in the direction of the woman helping herself to the bush tucker on offer. 'We've got some stock over at the gallery shop, just bring her over.'

Daniel raises an eyebrow. 'She's not my girlfriend, Annie.'

My smile stays in place as I accept a glass of wine from a waiter with a nod of thanks, wondering why both Davies brothers insist on calling me by names that I really don't like. 'Does *she* know that?'

He grins and winks at me. 'A man has needs.' I see a bit more of Dusty in Daniel than I'd like to and it takes me aback.

'How's your family?' I ask, changing the subject as casually as I can, trying to determine whether he knows about Dusty and I yet, whether it's come up in conversation between the brothers. I have to navigate this conversation carefully – I'm not dating the artist, which would be an actual problem, but dating the artist's brother doesn't exactly feel like it'll be accepted either.

'I haven't seen them for a while,' Daniel answers. 'Haven't been home for a few weeks now. My brother and I have both been travelling a bit. Me seeking artistic inspiration, and Dusty doing his my-little-pony gig.'

'That's not very nice,' I say, defensively. 'I'm sure he's as proud of what he does as you are of your work.'

'It's fine,' Daniel brushes it off. 'We tease each other all the time. He makes fun of my artsy-fartsy ways and I make fun of his cowboy drawl. We really love each other. It's harmless. Anyway,' he eyes me curiously, 'why do *you* care about my brother's feelings all of a sudden?'

My heart starts racing with nervousness as I recognise what might be the only opening I'll get. 'I've met him,' I blurt. 'Dusty, I mean.' Daniel raises his eyebrow again but doesn't say anything, so I forge on, trying to explain but not explain *too much*. 'When you and I first spoke, up in Warwick – my friends were going to the rodeo. That's why we were in town. Anyway, I met your brother there.' I glance away to where the speakers are getting ready to start, striving for nonchalance. 'We actually kind of hit it off.'

'Did you now?' Daniel's reply is cheeky.

'Mmm.' I hum noncommittally and sip some wine. 'I saw him down the coast a few weeks ago, too.'

I'm saved from having to disclose any further details as the speeches begin. I move to the side of the venue, away from Daniel, who has joined his date in the third row.

I opt to stand, to suss out who else is there from the local Black arts mafia. As I scan the space, Michael walks in via the yarning circle entry. He is a walking, talking example of a successful, urban Blackfella, the epitome of contemporary First Nations excellence wrapped up in what looks like a deadly new suit. He smiles, nods, and carefully and quietly makes his way to my side, pecking me on the cheek.

'Fancy seeing you here,' I whisper. Feels like this event is bringing everyone out of the woodwork. I hadn't mentioned this event during our morning runs, so I wasn't expecting to see him tonight.

Michael speaks quietly and quickly. 'My firm provides some financial support to the Chamber of Commerce to run workshops and mentorships,' he explains, nodding subtly to the banner with his firm's logo on it. 'One of our interns has an arts background and she does the architectural illustrations for us. She's a member of this network and I'm just here to support her and rep the firm.' He discreetly points to a young Murri woman sitting in the back row, looking a little nervous. 'This is more fun than architecture,' he whispers.

We both return our attention to where the chair of the chamber is thanking everyone for attending, then introduces some of the members of the network, including Daniel, who gets one of the biggest rounds of applause. I can't wait till the gallery opening; now more than ever I'm confident that choosing him as the spotlight artist was the best idea I've had since leaving Sydney.

My phone vibrates. I reach into my handbag and see that it's Dusty, but it'd be too rude to pull the phone out now. He'll have to wait, but my heart is happy that he's responded so swiftly.

After the event, Michael invites me to dinner at the pizza joint across from the gallery. 'So, Daniel Davies is going to be a big name, it seems.'

'Looks that way,' I answer happily. Michael's heard more than his fair share about Daniel's work during our morning runs and my hopes for what his art will bring to the gallery.

He sips his drink. 'What does he think about you and his brother?'

'He doesn't really know about it.'

Michael chokes slightly, then coughs to recover. 'Excuse me?'

'I mean, I've told him that I *know* his brother,' I rush to explain. 'Just . . . I haven't gone further into it.'

I can tell by his expression just how weird Michael thinks this is. Not-so-deep-down, I also know it's weird. And it's going to get a whole lot weirder when we see each other unexpectedly in Rocky. I try to justify myself anyway.

'Is it really my place to tell him everything? I'm not sure that it is. Daniel is my client, not my family.'

Michael scoffs slightly and says, 'Are you even Black, Annabelle? Of *course* it's your place to tell him. The Murri grapevine will share it anyway. I'm surprised he hasn't heard it from someone else already.'

'You're right, of course. But Dusty and I've kept it low-key. We've only seen each other at the rodeo and on the Gold Coast.' *Was keeping it low-key intentional or not?* I ask myself. 'I told Daniel that I met Dusty at the rodeo and then on the Gold Coast. He can figure the rest out. I'm not going to say, "I'm shagging your brother".'

Michael shakes his head wryly. 'Stay classy, Annabelle.'

I'm embarrassed. I value Michael's opinion and I don't want him to think less of me. 'I'm grateful for your friendship and honesty,' I say, and it's true. In the two months I've gotten to know him, I've felt more comfortable talking to Michael about a lot of personal moments in my life. Angel has Kev, and CJ and MJ live together, so they get to debrief constantly. Since moving back to Magandjin, I've seen only Michael on a semi-daily basis when we catch up in the mornings, and he's been an amazing ear and support. Our chats have given me cause to think about my actions, and I think he provides the emotional connection I've only been able to start considering with Dusty since the Gold Coast.

Now, he speaks matter-of-factly. 'If I were Dusty, or any other guy dating you, I'd be telling the world, so the fact he hasn't previously mentioned it to his brother –' He stops himself from finishing the sentence.

'What?' I prompt, already dreading the answer.

'Just be careful, Annabelle. Protect your beautiful heart and make sure you're not investing more than he is emotionally.'

There's something in the way that Michael cautions me that doesn't get me offside the same way that CJ, MJ, and Angel did, and I accept his caring words graciously.

'It's on me tonight,' I say as the bill arrives, a small act of gratitude.

As we leave the restaurant, the owner shakes Michael's hand and wishes him happy birthday.

'It's your birthday? How did the owner know and I didn't? Why didn't you tell me?'

'It's tomorrow, he's a family friend, and I eat here a lot, usually on my own,' Michael answers quickly, ushering me out the door, and clearly embarrassed by the attention. 'I don't like a big fuss made on my birthday, it's not my style.'

I just shake my head and start planning how to low-key celebrate with him. How old would he be tomorrow? I'm guessing 38 or 39. 'You *must* let me make you dinner, please, Michael. Just something to mark your born day. I won't take no for an answer.' I'm clearly determined and Michael knows me well enough now not to argue.

'That would be lovely, thank you.'

Later, I lie in bed and re-read Dusty's message over and over:

I miss my little bull rider. See you soon Sweetheart. XO

As I doze off, I replay Michael's comment about how other men would be telling everyone about who they were dating. I think about how much I want to see Dusty, and not just for the sex. I'm no longer bothered about his pet name for me, just that he's attentive and was thinking about me tonight, too. My head is about to explode with the confusion of it all, but I'm so exhausted, sleep finally takes hold.

\* \* \*

The next day, I race from the gallery at 5.30 pm, pick up a pre-ordered cake from The Barracks and walk in my door at 6 pm. Then I'm chopping, grating, and setting the table, a circle of activity while Thelma Plum wafts through my speakers. At 6.30 pm on the dot, Michael is knocking on the door. I'm a tad frazzled, but it's nothing a glass of bubbles won't fix.

'Happy birthday to you,' I start singing as he walks in.

'Something smells good,' he says.

'I've prepared a fun meal, hope that's okay. Just tacos, with freshly chopped tomatoes from our favourite market vendor, delish guacamole, and all the other trimmings. You take a seat, pour the bubbles, and I'll bring the mince and beans over.'

He moves to the table covered with all the colourful taco toppings in groovy bowls. We sit and fill our taco shells and talk and laugh. I get a bit tipsy, but Michael barely touches his champagne. Eventually, he sits back and rubs his stomach.

'They were the best tacos I have *ever* tasted,' he announces, tossing his serviette to the side.

I'm feeling very proud of myself. 'I'm really pleased to hear that. Do you want to know what the secret ingredient is?'

'Sure do,' he says. 'Then I can make my tacos taste as good as yours.'

'Don't be cross,' I say, 'but I used the roo mince I got at the markets.' As soon as I say it, I realise that I didn't really think this through. He told me he didn't want to eat roo, and I didn't ask any follow-up questions. Maybe it's his totem, but surely he would've said so at the markets if that were the case? Either way, though, I realise too late that I've basically tricked him. I'm just about to apologise when he speaks.

'Well, there you go. I was convinced to eat kangaroo without even knowing it, like cutting veggies into funny shapes for kids.'

'I'm so sorry, Michael. I thought it was a good idea at the time, but now I can see it was wrong and pretty stupid of me to deceive you. I'm an idiot sometimes.' I pause. 'Some might say a lot of the time.'

He stands up and walks over to me, plants a kiss on my cheek, and starts clearing the plates. The bubbly and the embarrassment make my face feel flushed. 'You're not stupid or an idiot,' Michael says calmly. 'You're a thoughtful, kind, generous woman who thought the only way I would eat roo was to camouflage it in tacos. And you were right, and I'm glad, because I love it, and I'll grab some myself next time we go to the markets.'

I know he is making light of it, but I am burning with

disgust in myself. It's not as bad as spiking a drink, but not much smarter either. 'You're not angry with me? I know I'd be pissed off if someone pulled a stunt like that on me.'

He shakes his head and I jump up with relief and gratitude, hug him quickly, and head to the fridge while he places the dishes in the kitchen sink. It's time for the cake, so I motion for Michael to sit back down when the table is cleared. I stick three candles into the chocolate mud cake and light them.

'Happy birthday to my deadly neighbour and friend,' I say with perfect sincerity and a smile. 'You deserve all good things today and tomorrow and all the days that follow.'

'A birthday poem!' he exclaims in delight, then blows out the candles and cuts the cake, and I truly hope all his wishes come true.

# CHAPTER EIGHT

Two weeks later, MJ, CJ, and I arrive into the mild May weather of Rocky. We've just picked up our hire car when our phones simultaneously ping with a message.

'Can someone please read it out while I set up Bluetooth?' I'm focussed on getting us out of the airport and into town without any hassles.

MJ laughs. 'It's Angel! She says, "Remember that the rules of any car journey are that the driver should just drive, focus on the road, and not kill anyone".' She keeps reading and informs us that the person riding shotgun (her) is responsible for assisting with navigation and being the DJ.

CJ giggles from the back seat. 'Apparently I am responsible for snack distribution.' She holds up chocolate and protein bars for us.

'I don't need your assistance with navigation, thanks, MJ,' I say, although my anxiety is building as I struggle to put the hotel address into Google Maps. My mind is fixed on getting to the hotel and the night ahead with Dusty and his family, and the chatter isn't helping. 'Okay, can we have just a little quiet for a minute?' I can hear the stress in my voice. In my periphery, I see CJ tap MJ on the shoulder. They know I'm nervous as hell about the weekend, but thankfully, they say nothing. Finally, the app seems to work out where we're supposed to go. 'Right, we are good to go. First stop, the hotel.'

We're only at the boom gate heading out of the airport when MJ screeches, 'Stop! Stop!'

'What the hell?' I slam the brakes in case there's a kid on the road I didn't see. 'What is it?' But MJ is out of the car and slamming the door behind her before I can stop her. She's running towards a bull installation to get a photo, followed by CJ shrieking about a selfie.

'It's not safe!' I shout out the window. The two women are by the bull before I can stop them. 'Hurry up, before security comes!' People beep their horns as they drive into the airport carpark and see my two friends acting like crazy tourists.

As they climb back into the four-wheel drive, MJ puffs, 'Sorry about that, totally forgot the first bull was at the airport. But we can tick The Droughtmaster Bull off the list!'

'You're both crazy!' I shake my head but smile, because their craziness and sense of freedom is just what I need right now to distract from my nerves.

MJ turns up the radio as brother-boy Troy Cassar-Daley sings out over the airwaves. For a few seconds, I feel calmer as we all sing along to the chorus of 'Dream Out Loud', which has become our anthem.

'Stop! Stop!' MJ screeches again. 'There's the next one.'

'You need to stop doing that, it's dangerous.' Not to mention I might go deaf before we get to the hotel. 'Don't you have notes there for us about passenger etiquette and safety? CJ, where's that lengthy itinerary you did for the rodeo with rules and topics and every other detail? We can use that now.'

'Please stop,' MJ says more gently. 'I really do want to get a full set of bulls if I possibly can.'

'It's in the roundabout, you nutter,' I laugh, remembering how much fun we girls used to have together on road trips and weekends away before I moved to Sydney. I know I need to loosen up. 'I suppose I could just go around a few times.'

I look in the rearview mirror. There's surprisingly little traffic, so I slow down and my tiddas jump out, racing across the road into the roundabout and laughing like naughty school kids. MJ takes a quick selfie with CJ for her socials, then swings her professional camera around and takes her time to get the perfect shot. I start beeping the horn. It feels like ten minutes of me driving round and round and round, and I'm starting to think there are cameras somewhere capturing it all and a fine will appear in the post sometime in the future.

They finally climb back in the car, MJ ticks Brahman Bull off the list, and we apparently now only have four more bulls to go.

'You're both crazy *and* have no shame, you know that don't you?' I say. 'And you only mentioned professional shots for your portfolio?'

'Yes, but the selfies are just for us! I'll wave my magic, they'll look a million bucks, and I might just make a TikTok of them.' She grins as she looks through the pics.

'As long as I'm not in any of them, agreed?'

'I'm not sure I've agreed to anything,' MJ sounds serious. 'Actually, I've got an idea about a photo of you trying to steal a bull's testicles. It's a thing here you know. Something we could take especially for Angel, perhaps.' She and CJ burst out laughing, and I know she's joking, but for the life of me I can't even crack a smile because I'm so nervous about meeting Dusty's family.

Before we arrive at the hotel, I've been forced to stop three more times for 'bull selfies' and long, drawn-out professional bull portraits. By the time we're done, my head is ready to explode.

'You will *never* see me in a bull selfie, ever,' I exclaim as we finally get to the hotel.

After we've checked in, I head immediately for the lift. 'I'm going to change and go for a short run. Need to move the legs a little, clear the head.'

'Try and find your sense of humour while you're out there,' MJ jokes lightly. 'Maybe it's over the river.'

'I will, I'm sorry, it's . . .' I stop before I confess that it's the emotional shift in what I feel for Dusty since our time on the Gold Coast and the growing intimacy between us that's freaking me out, on top of the nerves of meeting his family.

'They're going to love you,' CJ says, reading my mind. My friends go in search of the biggest steaks they can find and the biggest wines.

Fifteen minutes later, I'm in my running gear and heading along the Fitzroy River, stopping occasionally to take photos and imagine what life would've been like for the Darumbal people when the Ancestors walked their own uncemented paths, before the town introduced cattle, back when everyone across the land knew their totems, and animals were protected and cherished.

Weaving my way back into town proper in desperate search for a coffee, I find a bull mural on a wall in a lane, and think about MJ and CJ. They have been so supportive coming up for the weekend with me. I know I've been a grumpy bitch so far and it has to end. So, I take a selfie and send the pic in a text to the girls:

I'm sorry for being a cow. Please accept this bull.

\* \* \*

That night, as we stand at the bar of the Grand Corral Hotel, we go through the plan for the evening.

'You know the rules.' I sip my drink nervously.

'Yes, stay away from you unless you text the code word,' MJ recites.

'VEGAN!' we all exclaim simultaneously and laugh.

'I feel sick,' I say, up on my toes, trying to see into the arena. 'Oh god, I can see him, them – I'm going to vomit.'

CJ gives me a little shove. 'They're going to love you. And don't forget to mention Riverfire at my place. Dusty's more than welcome.'

'Wish me luck.' I take a deep breath and turn towards the door.

'You've got this, tidda!' MJ calls after me. 'You've got the brains and now you've also got the boots to match this mob.'

'They're going to love you!' CJ adds, one last time.

I play the line over and over in my head like a mantra as I show the bouncer my ticket: *They are going to love you, they are going to love you, they are going to love you.* It echoes as I try my best to do a casual, sexy saunter over to where Dusty stands. He has his back to me, but I'd know that butt anywhere. As I get closer, I see Daniel and a woman that must be their sister. Her eyes and cheekbones are incredibly similar to the Davies brothers.

'Hello,' I say softly, walking into the group.

Daniel does an exaggerated double-take. 'Fancy seeing you here, Annie!'

'Hi,' I say again nervously. I'm glad I gave Daniel the heads up, but it still feels a bit awkward.

Dusty's sister, Naomi, introduces herself. She is warm, chirpy, friendly, and leans in and gives me a peck on the cheek like you would at a family gathering, putting me at ease.

'I didn't think this would be your thing.' Daniel wobbles me off my axis again. I wish he would just stay quiet.

'I invited her.' Dusty puts his arm firmly around my waist. 'So you can just take that smile of yours, Danny Boy, and point it in any other direction but this one.' He kisses me hard on the cheek. It's awkward, but it's something.

There's silence for a second, then a roar as the crowds go crazy. An announcement comes through the loudspeakers about the event about to start, and people start to move to their seats in the huge indoor arena.

Naomi leads the way, Dusty behind, holding my hand as we head to what appear to be pretty good seats. I spot a man who looks like a much older, weathered version of Dusty and assume he's Mr Davies. He sits at the opposite end of the row to me.

As the crowd stands for the national anthem, I feel pressured once again not to make a scene, just as I did at the rodeo. When I'm at government events or representing any of my workplaces, I'll stand but not sing, and I opt for the same tonight. *A private protest is better than none*, I convince myself.

Dusty takes his hat off and belts out the words in fine tune and with pride, and I feel like I'm at some patriotic American sporting match. Blackfellas singing the anthem by choice has always confused me. I almost want to slap him with a pair of chaps. I close my eyes and wait for the moment to end, hoping that MJ and CJ can't see him. I've long been critical of a nation who only knows one verse of their anthem, but tonight I'm glad the crowd doesn't continue into the second.

As the masses take their seats again, Dusty puts his hand on my thigh, my heart settles, and the reality of where I am sinks in. I scan the arena in awe, confused, challenged, trying to understand the culture of bull riding and those who participate in and follow it.

'Let's hear it for the Red Dust Girls!' the MC yells, and two women in tight black leather pants, perfect boobs, and full lips stroll out to a wave of cheers. I momentarily contemplate Botox when I see how smooth their skin appears on the big screen, then look to my new boots, grateful that at least my toes aren't numb tonight.

'Now let's hear it for the cowboys of the PBA tour!' the MC bellows and another roar goes up. 'Coming out are the top bull riders in Australia right now. Say hello to Nathan Eppo from outback Queensland and Joe Windang from country Victoria.' The intros go on as the competitors are welcomed, each rider greeted by a burst of flames and another roar from the crowd.

During a lull in the excitement of the opening, there's a drinks order being taken. Dusty asks if I want a beer. Daniel gets up to follow him, and as he walks past me, I grab his arm and ask, 'Can you see if there's a low carb beer, please?'

'Sure, you and Dusty and low carb beer. Glad I have front row seats to watch it all.' Daniel walks off chuckling. Is he making fun of me, especially me and Dusty? I can't exactly race off after him to ask.

The opening event is a series of kids under 12 years old. The first young fella appears wearing a helmet and vest, and I'm fearful for his safety even with the protective gear on. I can't imagine ever wanting my kids doing something like this. I think back to my first conversation with Dusty, about how they all grew up living this life. It's as normal for them as playing footy or cricket, or going to the beach is for kids living on the coast.

The MC makes the announcement for the next event. 'First up is 19-year-old Joshua Davies from the Southern Downs against Big Thunder, make some noise!' Dusty and all his family are cheering for his nephew. Dusty sings out then lets rip the longest whistle I've ever heard. The man really has some interesting skills. I haven't heard a whistle like that since I was a kid and Dad would round up all the children when it got too dark to be playing in the street. For a moment, I feel a lump in my throat remembering Dad, who passed away too young, and wonder what he would make of Dusty. Is this the kind of man my parents would want to see me with?

When the bull throws Joshua, Dusty's hand clenches my thigh. I know that he's worried about the young fella, who gets up and limps at speed as the bull chases him to the fence. He's up and over it just in time, and then the entertainment *really* begins.

The MC is commentating every move. 'There's no bucking way he was going to catch that young fella, he legged it outta there! And now it looks like there's no bucking way Big Thunder is going to leave the ring!'

The crowd are laughing and cheering as Big Thunder steals the show, kicking up dust with his left hind leg, as if to charge, and seemingly loving every minute of the crowd's attention. The bull even walks to the camera behind the fence and eyeballs the cameraman, who steps back. It's the best part of the show for me, and from the texts coming in from the girls, they're in full agreement.

'Go Big Thunder!'

The standoff goes for a bit too long and eventually they bring in another bull who appears to encourage Big Thunder to leave. The audience cheers some more.

'Make some noise for the boys helping us out tonight,' the MC urges, and the venue erupts again, applauding the pick-up men who are responsible for directing the bulls and leading them to the exit.

I feel like I'm in a parallel universe. I'm obsessively watching the men on the fence who assist the riders as they prep, pulling the bulls' ropes and getting the animals angry, and then getting the riders' hands in place. My heart races whenever the gate opens and the crowd roars as the bull starts to buck immediately, the young rider looking like he's going to fly off like a cowboy ragdoll. I grab Dusty and bury my head in his shoulder.

My phone buzzes and I glance quickly at a selfie of MJ and CJ at what looks like the ladies' toilets, under a sign that says 'Heifers'. MJ is laughing, CJ looks cranky.

Meet us at the food stand.

I excuse myself and meet the girls in line for a veggie burger. They fire a dozen questions at me about the night so far.

'I think it's going okay,' I tell them. 'His sister is lovely, and I think Daniel is taking the piss, but I'm not sure. Dusty is being Dusty, haven't officially met the parents yet as they are at the end of the row of family, and my favourite part so far was Big Thunder owning the ring.' CJ wants to know if there's an itinerary for tomorrow. I pause, thinking on my feet. 'There will be, I'll give you the first meeting place before you go to sleep.' *Bloody hell*, I think to myself. Dusty will probably sleep in, and the girls will need breakfast, but I hadn't thought past getting naked tonight. 'I better get back. Here are the keys to the car – I'll go with Dusty, but text me later, okay?'

When I get back to the grandstand, everyone has shuffled seats and Naomi is on my right.

'Enjoying it?' she asks over the noise, gesturing widely to everything.

'Yes, I am, are you? And I'm sorry about your son.' Is that what you say? I have zero idea.

Naomi shrugs and smiles. 'We take the good with the bad, it's all part of the journey,' she says. 'We're going to the caves tomorrow. You should come, they're quite extraordinary.'

I'm grateful for the invitation. 'Sounds great,' I reply. 'Is it okay if my two girlfriends come too? CJ is a schoolteacher and will love learning about the place, and MJ's a photographer always looking for new and interesting things to capture.'

'More the merrier,' Naomi says and we agree to meet at the caves at 10 am. Our itinerary starts to write itself and I text my tiddas.

> We're going to the caves tomorrow morning. Meet you in the foyer at 8 for breakfast and debrief for 9.15 departure. We need to be there by 10 am.

When the event is over, a local band starts setting up, and Team Davies empty a good portion of the grandstand as we file out and gather in the bar. Daniel seems to have left without saying goodbye and I'm hoping that nothing has changed between us professionally. I really can't afford another personal mistake to ruin my current career path.

Next to me is Dusty's mum, who stands somewhat shorter than the lanky Mr Davies. She takes my hand. 'It's nice to meet you, even if it *is* the end of the night.' She turns to Dusty and says, 'We have to go, son, a lot of the mob are staying at our place. They'll be wanting cups of tea.'

'And your famous cookies, no doubt,' he says. She kisses him on the cheek when he leans down to her height.

Mr Davies shakes Dusty's hand, tips his hat at me, and smiles. No words spoken at all.

Naomi bypasses Dusty altogether and gives me a warm hug. 'See you in the morning and thanks so much for coming tonight.'

'Can't wait!' I tell her.

As we walk back to the car, I have a spring in my step. I've survived the bull riding, the national anthem, and meeting the family, which was far less dramatic than I expected. I realise belatedly that it was never going to be about me tonight. They were all here for Dusty's nephew.

'I'm excited about us going to the caves tomorrow,' I say, linking my arm with Dusty's.

'I won't be going, Sweedard,' he responds. 'That's for you and Nay and Danny Boy.'

I stop. 'But aren't we here together?'

'Yeah, but you know I like to sleep in the morning. You'll be in those caves and out again before I have my first durrie and Coke.'

I can feel disappointment rising. I love the morning, the prospect of a new day and what can be achieved, and Dusty wants to sleep it away. I shake my head and unhook myself from his arm.

He pulls me back into him almost immediately and kisses me softly on the mouth. 'Sweedard, don't be like that. We had a deadly night, didn't we? And I'm happy you and Nay get along. She doesn't have a lot of women around her, it's mostly just her and the men. I'm glad you want to go tomorrow, that'll make Sis happy.'

I can't argue with that. 'She said MJ and CJ could go too.'

'There you go, everyone wins. The girls have a day out and I get to sleep in. Anyway, I get the feeling that your friends don't like me. I mean, they haven't come near us all night.'

'What? Don't be silly! Why would you say that?' I can hear myself protesting too much. 'CJ made a point of reminding me to ask you to watch Riverfire at her place in a few weeks' time. She likes you, they all like you.'

He raises an eyebrow at me and I know I've done a shit job of convincing him. I wonder whether I should tell him they're as wary of him as they are of any man who comes into any of our lives, or that I instructed them to stay away tonight for fear they'd say something that might shake our new relationship.

'Please say you'll come down for Riverfire,' I say with a pout. The silence is deafening so I do the only thing I can think of to change the mood – I lean close, run my tongue along his bottom then his top lip, and whisper, 'Please come.'

'I'll come for you, Sweedard,' he says in a husky, seductive voice, and his kiss consumes me.

*\*\*\**

'Thanks for inviting us,' I say when we meet Naomi and Daniel in the morning. People are gathering as the tour of the caves is about to begin.

'How'd you enjoy last night?' Daniel asks, and I struggle to interpret his tone.

'It was a bit of a culture shock, to say the least,' I reply as casually as I can.

CJ hushes us as the young guide pulls the group together and launches into a brief history of the caves – beginning in the 19th century.

'Hang on,' MJ says out loud, and we exchange clearly gobsmacked glances about the glaring omission of an Acknowledgement of Country. History didn't begin when white people appeared somewhere on the land. CJ is quickly making notes on her phone for what I know will be a letter to Tourism Queensland.

'Unbelievable,' Daniel mutters and Naomi looks livid, but before anyone has the chance to interject, the group is moving along the path and into the caves.

We move single file through the caves and time passes quickly, until we're sitting quietly in pitch blackness in what is known as the cathedral. Leonard Cohen's 'Hallelujah' reverberates through the space as a female soloist sings the hymnal song. It's a spiritual moment and I feel the power of her voice move through my own body.

When the music ends, Daniel whispers, 'Miiesha did a show here and I heard it was incredible. I think she's coming back soon.' I know it would've been an extraordinary experience to see and hear the First Nations singer-songwriter from Woorabinda perform here, and I mentally note to check if there's a follow-up show planned.

Once we're back outside, Naomi suggests lunch at the pub and a debrief. We all agree, and less than ten minutes later, everyone's seated and Daniel and I head to the bar for drinks. As the barman pours, Daniel turns to me and at last drops the axe. 'So, you and Dusty, eh?'

I'm cornered. 'I told you we caught up on the Gold Coast. But really, my personal relationship with Dusty is separate from our professional arrangement, Daniel.' I can hear myself trying to justify something that shouldn't need it.

'I know,' he says.

'I don't want people to think I'm showing your work because –'

'You're sleeping with my brother?' He raises one eyebrow.

'Something like that,' I say sheepishly. 'I've had something like that happen in the past about a conflict of interest, and quite frankly, I can't risk that happening again.'

'I completely understand, but I also know that my work speaks for itself and that it's worthy to be hung in *any* gallery. So I don't think anyone will question that, regardless of your personal choices. Which I must say, are a little at odds with what I know about you so far.'

I'm a bit offended. 'At odds, how?'

'You're passionate about the arts. Dusty couldn't be more disinterested.'

'You don't have to like everything the same.'

'I've seen you almost gag when someone walks past you blowing cigarette smoke. So, I'm not sure how you're coping, because I do know that Dusty will not quit for *anyone*!'

Daniel's emphasis on *anyone* annoys me. 'I'm not just *anyone*!' I counter. 'And relationships are about give and take.'

'So it's a relationship, then? I'm impressed, and a bit surprised.'

'Why?' I sound defensive, but really, Daniel is no more surprised than the girls were.

'I just can't imagine what you talk about. Certainly not the politics of First Nations art, or the art of Western saddles.' He laughs and I'm annoyed.

I'm not sure why Daniel is so interested and asking so many questions, but I feel like I'm under the spotlight. And he's waiting for a response.

'I think you're getting a bit personal now, Daniel.' I smile to hide my discomfort. 'Dusty and I are like chalk and cheese, just like you and he are, but what we connect about is really between him and me.'

'All I'm saying is that I'm his brother and even *I* struggle to find common interests. And Dusty, well, he *will* try to please people he cares about, to his own detriment.' Daniel smoothly picks up four drinks from the bar, leaving me to grab only one while I try to read between Daniel's lines. As we walk back to the table, he says, 'Dusty aside, I'm glad you came, it gives Naomi some company.'

I smile at that. 'Dusty said something similar.' I stop myself from adding that maybe he might have more in common with his brother than he thinks.

On the drive back into town, I push the conversation with Daniel to the back of my mind. I'm looking forward to seeing Dusty and wondering what he has planned for the afternoon, when my thoughts are broken by angry words from CJ.

'I'm writing to Tourism Queensland and the newspaper about this morning. Truth-telling in tourism, that's what I'll lead with in my letter *and* my review of the caves. I can probably pull some words from the letter I wrote about the rodeo.' CJ is always practical in her activism, and I love her for it. She doesn't just talk about issues, she acts. 'I'll mention the Nurim Boardwalk on Mount Archer, and the public artwork inspired by Darumbal artist Ernest Garrett, too, just to show acknowledgement has been done locally elsewhere.'

MJ agrees vehemently. 'If you want them, I've got heaps of photos from other tourist sites around the country that show how acknowledgement signage can be done in a permanent way.'

We finish the drive in simmering silence and I'm thankful for the amazing women I have in my life. Strong, capable women who don't think truth-telling in this country is just about us wanting to rewrite history. None of us will accept anything less than honesty and accountability.

\*\*\*

'Wake up, my hot cowboy,' I whisper in Dusty's ear. 'It's past lunchtime already and you need to get out of bed. It's a gorgeous day.'

'Come here, Sweedard,' he mutters, and pulls me on top of him.

I can feel him through my knickers, and pull off my linen dress and bra and lean down to kiss him. We spend the afternoon making love in twisted, sweaty sheets, dozing off and on, only leaving to grab the food delivery from the hotel room door.

I awake alone from one of my post-session naps in the late afternoon. 'Hell, look at the time! Dusty?'

'Out here, Sweedard,' he sings out from the balcony, where he's smoking. It seems he's okay at a second-floor height.

'Oh, don't do that, we'll get a fine.' I linger in the doorway, away from the smoke, and try not to pull a face. 'I don't know how you can be so fit and yet smoke and drink Coke *and* beer nearly every day.'

He shrugs. 'Don't nag, Sweedard. That's not the sexy city lady I know and –' he pauses, and my heart skips a beat. Is he going to say he loves me? Is it too soon? Am I ready to hear it? Do I even want to fall in love?

Instead, he reaches out, takes my hand, gently pulls me to his lap, his lips against mine. 'Know and want to kiss.'

I push him gently away and move to the other balcony chair. 'Cigarette breath. You know the rules.' At least I can tell the girls that I'm not what my old aunts used to call 'dicklashed'. I laughed the first time I heard it, when they were talking about one of my cousins who had been completely in thrall to a fella because he was so good in the sack.

He pulls out some gum. 'You're ruining a romantic moment, Sweedard. I thought you women liked romance.'

'*You're* the one who smells like an ashtray.' It's out before I can stop myself. Have I wounded him? I watch as Dusty chews his gum furiously, then takes it out and sticks it to his Coke bottle sitting on the outdoor table.

He stands up and moves towards me, leading from the hips. 'Don't be like that, Sweedard.'

'Dinner is booked for 7 pm,' I say after he finally lands a kiss. 'We haven't got long.'

A little later, we're holding hands and walking along the main street. I feel comfortable, happy in the lovemaking afterglow, but a tad annoyed with myself for wasting so much energy on being so anxious before the trip. I know there's no chance of changing someone like Dusty at this stage in life or in our relationship. *Or is there?* I ask myself. Either I'll have to hang in there for any changes over time or accept him as he is right now.

As I step off the curb, my phone vibrates with a message from MJ:

**Have fun, we're off exploring, found some friends.**

She's sent a selfie with another bull and two fellas who look like they've won the jackpot. I respond quickly:

**And you too! Can't wait for the debrief on the way home.**

I can see the restaurant up ahead, but Dusty tugs me gently to the right as he steps towards the pub.

'Where are you going?' I ask, confused.

'The Criterion,' he responds. 'Aren't we having dinner?'

'Yes, but we're not going there.'
'But we *always* go to the Criterion.'
'Do we?'
'Well, we went in Toowoomba,' he says confidently.
'*I* didn't go to the pub in Toowoomba with you.'
'Ah, Sweedard, maybe we didn't go there, but we can go to the Criterion here.'

I stop in my tracks and glare at him.

'*And* when I visit you in Brisbane.'

I let go of his hand. 'Back up a step. You're having pub dinners with other women?'

'With other people, sure. Man's gotta eat,' he points out. 'No need to do it alone when there's company to be had.' He tilts his head and a smile twinkles in his eyes. 'Are you *jealous*, Sweedard?'

'Me? Ha! I don't have a jealous bone in my body,' I lie. These other women probably share a ciggie with him and eat mountains of meats and drink Coke and UDLs by the case. The mood has changed, or at least *my* mood has changed, and I find myself snapping, 'Do you think you can stop calling me "Sweedard" like I'm a random bogan and actually call me by my name? Or is that what cowboys usually call their girlfriends?'

*Shit! Did I just call myself his girlfriend? Quick, backpedal, backpedal!*

Dusty doesn't seem fazed. 'No, *cowboys* call their *girlfriends* "Darlin",' he drawls. 'But *you're* special.' He takes my hand again and pulls me back close to him, and I realise he's using seduction to try to end the argument before it starts. I can't judge him because I did the same thing just yesterday. 'I wanted to give you a special name,' he says cheerily.

His sweet words make me feel like the ultimate bitch, and I force away any jealousy and insecurity about his hypothetical pub dinner companions. 'In that case, "Sweedard" it is!' I kiss him hard on the lips, then lead the way back towards the Italian restaurant I've booked.

Dusty remains chirpy, holding my hand firmly as we walk the few extra metres down the road.

I start to worry that he'll be out of his comfort zone and wish I'd just gone to the pub after all. But to my surprise, Dusty is his usual friendly self, speaking pleasantly to the waitress escorting us to our table. He's so easy-going, it makes me feel that I am even *more* difficult to please. *I am not high maintenance, I am top shelf, and there's a difference.* I remember the mantra my girl gang have always used when anyone suggests we can't keep a man because we're too much work. *I am worth the work*, I tell myself as Dusty holds out my seat for me. Looks like chivalry is alive in Rocky.

'You okay?' I ask as he tucks his own chair in, his booted feet poking through to my side of the table.

'I'm fine and dandy, Sweedard. As long as I can get a steak, I'll be good as gold. You know I'm a man of simple tastes.' He looks around the restaurant with a smile on his face. 'This place looks all right. Good choice.'

'I'll check out the Criterion back home and maybe we can go there when you come for Riverfire, yes?'

'Whatever you want, Sweedard,' he replies as he looks at the menu. 'How was your little trip to the caves with Danny Boy and Nay?' he asks without looking up.

'Really interesting,' I begin excitedly, grateful to have a meaningful yarn with him.

'That so? When I went, it was just old, dark rocks and stuff.'

The waitress delivers a basket of garlic bread to the table.

'Well yes, it's dark and old,' I say as we both take a piece. 'But I learned so much, about limestone rocks and how the fig trees burrow through them. And that there's literally *thousands* of bats there.'

'Yeah, Nay told me there were 23,000. She loves a bit of trivia.' Dusty reaches for another piece of bread. 'I bet Danny Boy was spooked by the darkness. He's such a wuss sometimes.'

I frown. 'That's not very nice.'

Dusty waves a hand briefly. 'I'm just saying I can't imagine he sat there alone in the dark without a panic attack. He can be a very fragile, little artsy-fartsy fella.'

I can feel an argument brewing again. 'No, pretty sure Daniel thought the experience was spiritual.'

'And what about you?' he asks. 'Were you scared of the dark? Did you have to hold Danny Boy's hand?'

*Is he jealous now?* 'I loved it in the cathedral. It was like being underwater, very soothing, very relaxing. I'd like to go back again.' I kind of hope Dusty will offer to go with me, but he says nothing.

I glance around the restaurant and wonder what other people see when they look at us together. Do we look awkward as a couple? Do we even look like a couple?

'So, a good day then?' he asks, apparently unaware of the direction my mind is spiralling.

'Mostly. But we all agreed that it was shitty that there was zero reference to the local mob here. Not even an acknowledgement of whose Country we were on when the tour started.' I take another piece of bread. 'It's not that hard, really. And, Dusty, they should've done it at last night's event as well,' I add.

'You three are all the same,' he says casually.

I stare him down. 'What's that supposed to mean?'

'You, Nay, and Danny Boy. Why do you have to make everything political?'

'You call it political, Dusty. I call it reality, truth-telling, and it's respectful. And quite frankly, knowing whose Country you're on is basic knowledge, or should be. The kids CJ sometimes teaches in primary school know more than many of the adults I've come across lately.' I take a sip of water. 'Those caves are supposedly over 300 million years old, but some European bloke somehow *discovered* them? Please. Do they honestly think that no Darumbal people saw them in the 60,000 plus years they were here before whitefellas?'

He sits looking at me, his face giving absolutely nothing away. I continue because I can't stop myself.

'All they needed to mention was something, *anything* about the fact that Blackfellas have lived here for millennia, that we *still* live here. This is history. *Our* history.' I gesture from me to him and back again, across the table. 'We're always being forgotten, as if this country started when white people arrived.'

'Not all whitefellas are bad, you know.'

'I'm not saying they are. My father's side aren't Black. And they're some of the best humans you'll ever meet.'

'Well, there you go,' Dusty says as if he's won the argument I don't even want to have.

'Yes, but they also know the history of Australia as a country, and the story of my mother's Country, and how colonialism continues to impact us, rendering us invisible. Just like the Darumbal mob were today, somehow written out of the story of the caves. Doesn't that bother you?'

When Dusty shrugs, I can feel tension building in my neck. My face is flushed, and I realise he must be able to see it when he reaches over and puts his calloused hands atop my shellacked fingernails. 'Don't get upset, I'm listening. I may not read, Sweedard, but I'm a good listener. I listen to my old people when they talk. And because of them, I know the stories of the land I come from, where I still live, but . . .'

'But what?'

'But can you say the same thing about *your* land and Country? I mean it's all well and good to get crankypants up here, but what about your own mob? What are you doing to raise awareness about issues on your *own* Country? You live a thousand miles from your family, your land.'

That stings. Dusty's right, but I'm not conceding that to him, not today. I'm too angry. I take a deep breath and say, 'You're right, Dusty, I don't live home on Country, and maybe it's selfish, but I can't follow my dreams in the arts down there. Not enough opportunities for curators, so I moved away, but with the blessings of my Elders, and they are the only people I'm answerable to.' I hear a quiver in my voice as I think of my Nanna Sony and Aunty Elaine and their decades of support for all the younger mob chasing dreams in ways the old people couldn't.

Dusty is listening, waiting, so I continue.

'Justice for mob anywhere is justice for us all, and just because this isn't my land, doesn't mean I can't raise awareness here too.'

'Okay,' is all he offers.

'All I am saying is at the bare minimum, they could let visitors know whose Country they're on. It's not that hard,' I insist.

I see a smile in his eyes and a big grin sweeps across his face, then a chuckle.

'What's so funny?' I ask defensively.

'Sometimes I think you're dating the wrong brother.'

I feel deflated.

'It's just that you and Daniel think so much alike,' he continues, trying to soothe me. 'Care about the same things and get upset over the same things.'

'Does that mean you don't care? And that you don't agree with me at all?'

'I do things different in the country to you in the city,

Sweedard, that's all. You lot make a lot of noise, and go on marches and that's great, that's important. Of course it is. But me, I'm living the quiet life, just trying to *live* in peace. Anyway,' he says. 'What's that saying, make love not war?' He takes a bite of bread and chews slowly.

I suck down the urge to argue, to say that we aren't at war, but we *are* meant to be on the same side about Black stuff. But I don't want to completely ruin our dinner and hate myself momentarily for wanting to abandon this argument, when he continues unexpectedly.

'You may think I don't appreciate Daniel's work, but I do. I know his art is his way of making a statement. Your work is your way. My way is to have quiet conversations, like this. Because we all learn differently, and so we need different ways to get messages across, just like your artists do it differently.' He smiles as he takes another bite of bread.

I'm seeing a different side of Dusty and my heart falls a little deeper into his as all the tension drains out of my body at his thoughtful words.

He picks up the menu. 'Now, what's this ozzo bucko? Sounds like something a cowboy should eat, eh?'

# CHAPTER NINE

> Want to run in the morning?

I text Michael as soon as I'm unpacked and finished preparing for the week ahead. When he doesn't respond, I belatedly send another text.

> Sorry, I meant, hello, how are you?

When he hasn't responded by 8 pm, I begin to worry. We don't usually go for more than a few days without texting or speaking. I lean over the balcony to see if there's a light on upstairs in his flat, but it's in darkness, so I don't bother going upstairs. At last, my phone pings.

> Hey, hey, welcome home. I was out all day, then a show tonight at QPAC. On way home now. Love to run in the morning, I've been lazy this weekend. LOL

I can't imagine Michael ever being lazy – he seems always on the go – but I'm happy to be back on routine.

As the sun rises, we set some cardio goals, and between each 100 m sprint, I tell Michael about Dusty's smoking and the national anthem, Naomi being super kind and welcoming, the bull selfies MJ insisted upon, the weird conversations with Daniel, the frustrating argument with Dusty about the caves, and the strange, sweet turn that ended it.

Michael listens, as he always does, like a personal trainer and a therapist wrapped into one. 'Does Dusty realise how special you are?' he asks at last.

I immediately feel the need to defend my cowboy. 'He treats me like I'm the best thing in his life, really. It's just that we're so different. He's so country and there are moments when he makes me feel like I'm so far removed from my own land that it's embarrassing.' I recall his comments from dinner. 'Those differences bother me, not him,' I clarify. 'I don't know, maybe I just need to be easier going.'

Michael stops in his tracks. 'You think being easy-going landed you one of the most important cultural roles in this state?'

I know he's right. Being focussed and determined, not giving up on what I know is right, standing up for every challenging artist, artwork, and issue when public opinion or local politics may have gotten in the way, *that's* what's gotten me where I am professionally today. 'Should the same standards apply for my personal life?' I answer his question with one of my own.

'Just my opinion,' he says, 'but I would say that they absolutely should.'

We walk back to our building, drenched in sweat. I love our morning runs for both my mental health and for our friendship.

'Are you going to keep seeing Dusty, then?' Michael asks as we catch our breath.

'He's coming to Magandjin next weekend for Riverfire,' I tell him. 'I suspect he's not seen anything like it before. But then, I shouldn't assume anything, because he surprises me all the time.'

Michael nods. 'I'd never seen anything like it before moving back here. I'm not a fan of fireworks, to be honest. We still have unhoused people sleeping under the Kurilpa Bridge and along the riverfront all year round. We can't afford to provide to house them, but we can afford to light up the sky they have to sleep under every night? Maybe sponsors could put the dosh towards supporting assisted accommodation in the city instead.'

'I've never thought of that, but you're right.' I resolve to talk to MJ about how we can raise awareness via our numerous social platforms.

Dusty would probably call Michael's advocacy for the homeless of Magandjin a political stand, but I know it's trying to put empathy in action. It's demonstrating a sense of humanity, not a political statement. I'm feeling torn as I walk into my apartment. Riverfire, the wasteful expense of government money, homelessness. Is this the best way to welcome Dusty into my life here in Magandjin?

I sigh heavily. It's the only welcome I've got right now, so I'll go with the flow for the sake of our relationship.

* * *

A light tap on my screen door alerts me to Dusty's arrival. He's early, and I've just stepped out of the shower. I'm surprised to see him in blue rather than black jeans and a checked shirt that looks more department store than showground stall. His boots must be his non-rodeo Sunday-best, and I feel like he's made a special effort for his special lady. A hot rush rises up my body.

'Now *this* is a welcome,' he says with a wide smile, kicking the front door shut behind him and gently tugging the fluffy towel off me and tossing it down the hallway.

The welcome session is quick and then we're dressed and on our way to Kangaroo Point, feeling very loved up. We arrive at MJ and CJ's apartment in the early afternoon, just down from Eagle Street Pier, with the perfect view of the fireworks to come.

'If I didn't like Paddington so much, I'd move over here, CJ,' I tell her as we walk in. 'The view is incredible.'

'We like it. And being able to walk along the riverfront to the city through the gardens is pretty great.' CJ explains to Dusty, 'If you walk to the left, you get to New Farm. That's the direction of the airport.'

MJ joins in. 'And see that sandstone building?' She points it out. 'That's Customs House.'

I wonder if it's obvious to Dusty that the girls are really trying hard to include him. My heart fills with love for my besties.

'The NAIDOC ball is going to be at Customs House in a few weeks,' MJ continues. Angel and Kev put out some treats from their health food store on the table as MJ tells us all the details about the uni students pulling the entire event together. She's going to be the photographer on the night.

My brain is ticking over about getting us all there, including Dusty. 'The gallery could get a table. Do you want to come?' I look at Angel and Kev, then CJ.

They're into the idea, and dresses and shoes are discussed as a matter of priority.

'Dusty?' I'm nervous to ask him in front of the others.

His hand on my butt, Dusty doesn't hesitate. 'Sweedard, if you want me to go, then I'll go.' I'm so glad the others can see Dusty's affection for me.

'Cinderella is going to the ball!' I announce. 'I'll sort it all out first thing Monday.'

'Speaking of NAIDOC,' CJ is bouncing with excitement, 'the school's having a NAIDOC week trivia night fundraiser for the local community centre, the night before the march. I'd love you all to come!'

We're all in, of course. I offer to donate something from the gallery, MJ will take some photos for the local paper, and Angel will make a few of her incredible cakes.

As the first of the fireworks begin, the others gather on the balcony, but Dusty chooses to stay behind. I walk over, thinking it's his discomfort with heights. 'We can see them from here, but the view's just a bit better out there,' I tell him, holding his hand.

'It's okay, Sweedard,' he says. 'Not a huge fan of fireworks, even the displays at the New Year's Eve rodeo.'

'Because they cost so much?' I ask, recalling Michael's complaint.

'Cost to the environment, yes. I'm a bit surprised you're into them?'

Now I'm surprised that *he's* surprised, and Dusty can see it on my face. He explains in a low voice. 'I remember you telling me some of your friends are vegans and I'm guessing they're all environmentalists too, like Danny Boy. So how can they also support fireworks?'

'I actually hadn't given it a lot of thought,' I admit.

'Fireworks create highly toxic pollutants that poison the air, water, and soil, and that makes that river below there lethal to birds and fish and other wildlife, not to mention people's pets and livestock. The pollution from fireworks lasts for hours or days on end.' Dusty speaks in a tone I've not heard from him before. It's the first time I've seen him completely serious – and, dare I say, *political* – about something other than horses and cattle, and I kind of love it.

'How do you know all of this?' I thought Daniel said that Dusty didn't care about the environment, but he clearly does. Since Rocky, I've been realising that he just cares about things very differently than I'm used to experiencing in my circles.

'My mate Johnno works for the CSIRO and he's the smartest bloke I know,' Dusty says. 'He reckons there's research on how fireworks impact humans, too. He talks about this stuff all the time. I've picked up some of it when we're out for a steak and a beer.'

Now I'm confused. 'But, Dusty, why did you come if you feel so strongly about fireworks?'

'To see you, Sweedard, of course.' And he slides his arm around my waist to pull me close to his side, just as Angel comes in off the balcony, interested to know what the conversation is about.

Dusty is on a roll now, and tells us about being in the US for a campdraft a few years ago and seeing the Fourth of July fireworks. He watched the news the next day and the reporter had said the fireworks introduced something like 42 percent more pollutants into the air than could be found on a normal day. Angel is gobsmacked and appalled at this new knowledge, as I am.

CJ and the others come in at the tail end of the conversation. 'Aren't they so pretty?' she says.

This sets Kev off on his own fireworks lecture. He's got a background in chemistry, so he describes that the prettiness we like comes from things like zinc, copper, and sodium, and all those chemicals and the dust are pollutants that settle on the landscape. 'If you go for your run tomorrow, Annabelle, you should look at what it's like down there.' He nods towards the balcony.

I hadn't pegged Dusty and Kev as a likely pair, but the two of them end up chatting quietly for most of the evening.

Back at my apartment that night, there's no more conversation about the fireworks or the environment. It's as if Dusty has said his piece and moved on, making peace not war, but still getting his message across. As an overthinker who dwells *a lot*, I admire his capacity to let things go.

When we wake in the morning, we're both quiet, and lovemaking is slow, almost gentle. *Landline* is on in the background as we eat breakfast on the balcony. I can't bring myself to do a bacon fry-up, but my man's plate is full of eggs, tomatoes, spinach, mushrooms, halloumi, and corn fritters I've made myself. I make good use of Michael's weekly gift of herbs, too.

Before he digs into the mountain of food in front of him, he takes some gum from his mouth and wraps it in a serviette.

'That's different,' I say, with a slight frown.

'Nicotine gum,' he says with a smile as he carves up his mushrooms.

*Nicotine gum*, I repeat to myself. My man is changing, for me. My heart swells.

Dusty plants a kiss on my lips and tells me his brekky is delicious, even without the bacon.

Michael's voice sings out, startling us both. 'Something smells good!'

'Good morning! We're just having some breakfast,' I call back, leaning over the railing to look up to him.

'Oh, sorry, forgot you had company.'

'Michael, this is Dusty. Dusty, Michael.' I'm happy that my two favourite guys finally get to meet.

'Hi Dusty, welcome to our hood,' Michael leans further over his balcony to throw Dusty a friendly wave.

'G'day,' Dusty waves back with a half-smile.

'I'll pop up later with some veggies from the market – I've got too much here, even after this big brekky,' I tell Michael.

'Sounds great, I'll catch you later.' As he disappears, I sit back down.

'So that's your city-boyfriend then?' Dusty teases.

'Shhhh, Michael is my *friend*. We train together a few mornings a week. He's very cool.'

'He looks like a male version of you.'

'What's that mean?'

'Black, city, hip, tidy, fit.'

'I'll take tidy as an unearned compliment,' I chuckle, looking at the mess my flat is this morning.

'As long as it's just veggies you're running upstairs?' Dusty raises an eyebrow.

I watch Michael's Tesla pull out of the driveway and head towards the city. 'We're just *friends*.'

When we're back inside, Dusty comes up behind me, slides his hands around my midriff, and nuzzles into my neck. 'I better get going, Sweedard.'

I walk him to his dusty, well-worn ute on the street, lightyears away from his brother's artwork-on-wheels. 'I'll see you in a few weeks for the ball?' I lean in the window and kiss him passionately goodbye.

'Look forward to it, Sweedard. Say goodbye to that

fella upstairs for me,' Dusty chuckles as he pulls out from the curb.

\* \* \*

Emails fly back and forth over the next few days as I try to organise the table for the ball at short notice and finalise all the details for the gallery opening. There are two weeks till the ball and four weeks till the opening, but organisation is one of my strengths. CJ is queen of schedules in our group, but I'm the queen of spreadsheets and to-do lists. I'm confident that it will all come together – I've planned everything down to the last detail.

Dusty's morning texts have slowed down, as have the phone calls, but I'm not too concerned. The depth of our conversation during Riverfire has moved our relationship to a whole new level. It's taken a turn, a good turn, from camping out on Sexy Street to a mansion on Sexy-and-Significant Street. The honeymoon isn't over, I tell myself. It's just gotten more real.

A few days before the ball, my tiddas are messaging furiously about our outfits on our group chat. Angel writes:

> I decided to wear white because I am an angel of course.

She's sent a photo of herself in a slinky white silk frock, skimming her curves in a way I've never seen before. She looks amazing.

I joke:

No crocs then Angel?

She replies:

Haven't decided on shoes but seeing as Kev and I never got married I thought I could kill a few birds, be an angel and a bride all in one. Kev's even hiring a suit, couldn't get him in a tux. But a suit! Can you believe it?

I laugh. My cousin is always keen to get the best bang for her buck. Considering how amazing she looks in that silk gown, I don't blame her for wanting it to be her wedding dress as well. I send my own pic next.

I'm wearing this black velvet dress. I like the cut-outs on the shoulders and the fishtail hem. And I've got silver shoes. Dusty's wearing a black suit, and I've got a tie from a collection we've just taken on by a Wiradyuri artist. Hope he's not planning on his boots!

MJ sends a pic in an electric blue, full-skirted midi dress with a halter neck and plunging neckline. She has a gold shoe on her left foot and a silver on her right.

Which shoe, ladies?

The verdict is two votes for silver and one for gold.

Finally, CJ sends us a selfie in a long, rainbow, strapless dress with purple pumps, looking stunning. With her hair and makeup done, she'll look more than a million bucks – we all will.

The conversation ends there, and I decide to put on my whole look for the ball and send a pic to Dusty:

You like? I can't wait for the ball. With you!

I get changed back into my regular clothes and get started cleaning my flat for Dusty's arrival when he messages me back:

I like, Cinderella, I like. I'll get there Saturday after 4 pm. Okay?

I'm smiling from the inside out when I write back:

Perfect! I'm busy till then. XO

I still have to get my hair, makeup, and nails done. My shellac has all but peeled off – I've been so busy at work that there's been little time for self-care. Everything is falling into place just as I want it.

\* \* \*

Tonight is CJ's NAIDOC Murri trivia night and we've had a blast workshopping a name for our team. We settled on #TeamDeadlies. Angel's hand-painted some tees for us and we look flash all matched up on table 4 at the front of the school hall.

We smash round one with questions about David Unaipon, Oodgeroo Noonuccal, the Warumpi Band, Ash Barty, Buddy Franklin, and Albert Namatjira. Although being competitive is not a Murri or Koori value, we're having too much fun and screeches of laughter echo across the hall. Every few minutes, table 4 is being shushed by the MC and that makes us all the louder.

We're not struggling in the second round, but I want an excuse to message Dusty, so I send a couple of the questions his way. He responds with a shrug emoji to the first and doesn't respond to the second. The three hours we're at the event could feed my soul for the year, and it's another reminder why NAIDOC Week is my favourite time of year.

I collapse into bed around 11 pm still chuckling to myself, feeling blessed. I text Michael, knowing that I won't have time to run in the morning.

> Hey there! I'll have to pass on a run in the morning. Will probs see you at the march though, yes? Sleep well.

He responds seconds later:

> Absolutely. See you there. Sweet dreams. M.

I sleep like a log and wake to a clear blue sky. The sun is up, but there's a winter chill in the air. I'm out the door fast and into the gallery for an early meeting, then head to Parliament House for speeches and the march. It's freezing cold and the wind is biting when my team arrive at the meeting spot, and Angel joins us. MJ is taking photos, but CJ is at school, coordinating a special assembly. The video she sends through of the students singing, dancing, performing poetry and skits makes me teary, and I think my gorgeous friend must be exhausted. We make a little video of support and send it back to her before the march starts.

I see Michael about 15 metres in front of me in an 'Australia: Drive it like you stole it' tee, holding the Murri flag and loudly chanting 'Black Lives Matter. Get Up, Stand Up, Show Up', revving up the people around him. I can't tell if they're his colleagues or just the mob he's in the middle of. I decide not to try to catch up to him – I'll see him at the ball, and we can debrief the speeches and the march then. Then again, with Dusty there, talking politics might *not* be a good idea.

I take some pics and footage to post on TikTok and send a couple to Dusty, then start to second-guess myself. I know he's not interested in this side of my life, of what I think should be *his* life, too. I sigh, still unable to really understand his position, and send a flood of pics to the mob back home instead.

After an early night, I roll out of bed on Saturday before sunrise. I've got buckets of energy, excited about seeing Dusty and everyone looking gorgeous, ready to party and celebrate all that is deadly in our community. Michael and I race to the markets and grab our weekly greens, and then I run in circles doing some work that can't wait till Monday. I'm finally at the salon getting my hair blow-dried after the best head massage I've ever had, when my phone pings. It's Dusty.

> Leaving home now, see you soon Cinderella. Hope these match your glass slippers.

He sends a photo of a pair of black dress shoes and I feel a hot rush. I know he's bought them for me. I reply:

> My prince's attire will match Cinderella's perfectly. Everyone is looking forward to seeing you.

Dusty responds a few minutes later:

> Everyone? At Riverfire the only genuine one there was Kev. I'm sure your friends were trying hard with me.

I think carefully about my response:

> All my friends are genuine Dusty, and you're only saying that because Kev agreed with you.

But I know he's right about the girls trying. I finish our conversation with:

> Now hurry up and get here. But drive safely. X

At 4.30, the makeup artist has finished my face and I head home. Michael and I pull into the carpark at the same time.

'Hey there!' Michael walks to my car as cheerful as ever in his gym gear. 'Getting my deadly choices in before tonight,' he says, taking a long sip from his drink bottle. 'You look gorgeous, Miss NAIDOC here we come.'

I laugh, but I'm grateful for the compliment. 'I'm so excited. Dusty will be here soon. We'll meet you there, okay?'

'Sounds like a plan. Tux is waiting to be worn and the shoes are ready for the dance floor.' He step-shuffles away singing something from the 80s and I follow behind up the stairwell.

Dusty hits traffic so I'm already dressed when he finally arrives, but I'm calm, or at least trying to be. I walk carefully in my heels to the door with a glass of bubbly.

'Oh, Sweedard, you are the most beautiful woman I have ever seen!' I feel like the most beautiful woman ever. I wish I felt like this every day. He pulls me in for a kiss, and I respond as passionately as I can without mucking up my near-perfect makeup before shooing him to the bedroom to get ready.

'Okay, okay, plenty of time for that when we get home. There are towels out for you, and I can't wait to see you in your suit!'

He walks off whistling and I love that it all seems so easy and natural between us. Dusty is quick to dress, and when he re-enters the living room, he looks so handsome,

I just want to tear his suit right off him. 'Seriously, you belong on a billboard in Hollywood, not at a student ball in Brisbane!'

He laughs as we head out the door.

When we arrive at Customs House, there's a red carpet leading up the stairs. I'm so proud to have Dusty as my date – not just my plus one, but the man I'm going home with, the man in my life. I want to introduce him to everyone, but I know this is still a big thing for him, in a suit, at the ball. I tame my excitement and stick close to him.

CJ arrives at the same time, stunning as always with a smile that captures the warmth and happiness she always radiates. Seeing her reminds me of all the beautiful people in my life.

'And hello,' MJ appears with her camera, clicking like the paparazzi. She moves in close to Dusty and me, snaps a photo and grins widely at the shot. 'Now *this* should go straight to the pool room, don't you think?' She shows us both the photo and I'm thankful she's making such an effort with Dusty.

'*The Castle* is one of my all-time favourite movies, seen it at least a dozen times,' Dusty tells me as he takes my arm in his, escorting me the old-fashioned way. The ballroom is decorated beautifully with native floral arrangements on each table and gold table runners and bunting, gold to celebrate Black excellence.

Once seated at a table to the left of the room, I move the place cards so that Kev is next to Dusty, seeing as they hit it off during Riverfire. Dusty is on my right, CJ is on my left. Daniel is surprisingly sans date and is sitting next to Michael, opposite Dusty, and two of my gallery staff make up the rest of the table, but they're already off roaming the room, catching up with mob of their own. I see some Aunties in the distance having their photos taken and remember the deadly NAIDOC balls at the Gundagai Services Club in years gone by. I smile thinking about all the Aunties dancing in circles, usually in long red or black dresses. It's moments like these I miss my mob the most.

There's no time to feel too sad though, because I'm so happy to be sitting next to my tuxed-up-billboard-looking bloke, a far-cry from the cigarette sucking, Coke drinking, black denim-clad cowboy I first met.

MJ waves the run sheet at us. 'Speeches are about to start,' she tells everyone, then mutters sotto voce in my ear, 'and you better keep an eye on your neighbour, cos I might just take him off for a private photo shoot.'

'I absolutely think you should do that! He does look a 10 tonight, doesn't he?' We both look over at Michael who is in an animated discussion of the menu with Daniel.

The room falls silent, and everyone listens as local language flows freely from an Elder's lips, as it would've before colonisation, before the brutal land grab that's often forgotten when sitting in the sandstone building we're celebrating in tonight. When the welcome is over, two dance troupes take the stage, singing and performing to music that is millennia old, songs and dances that have been passed on from generation to generation to generation. The richness of my own culture fills me with strength and gratitude for the life I enjoy today – the arts, my beautiful friends and family, the chance to be part of such a meaningful event in Magandjin. And Dusty.

When the student reps take the mic to address their peers, I see younger versions of me celebrating culture, diversity, university life, and just being with the mob. I join in the standing ovation for the young Murri doctor when his dinner speech inspires the hundreds there to celebrate – academics, Elders, and students alike. That's when I notice that Dusty has eaten his bread roll and mine, and is about to reach for Kev's. 'Everything all right?' I ask him quietly.

'Yeah, just hungry. It was a long drive. When's dinner coming?'

He's looking towards a waiter, I assume to wave him over, so I reach for his hand and hold it firmly under the table.

'Dinner will be served shortly and they don't serve drinks during the speeches,' I explain quickly. I can see Daniel watching us both from across the table, but I can't read his expression.

Between courses, we watch the award ceremonies, and Dusty talks mainly to Kev, about the weather, I think. When we finally get the main course, he hoovers his meal like he hasn't eaten in days.

'Are you having a good time?' I whisper.

'Yeah, Sweedard. Kev is the real deal, isn't he?'

'Yes, he is.'

As they clear the dinner plates, my heart is full, and when the music starts, I really want to get on the dancefloor.

'Shall we dance?' I nudge Dusty. But Dusty tells me that his legs are tired from riding and stays seated.

'Come on, you two, the dancefloor is heaving!' MJ calls over the music. 'Look, Angel's already got her shoes off.' She points to Angel and Kev on the dancefloor busting dance moves unseen since the 70s. I'm in a time warp and I love it.

I look at Dusty, and he smiles and waves towards the dancefloor. 'Go dance!'

CJ and I are up and sashaying our way to the dancefloor, arms in the air, singing along to Yothu Yindi's 'Treaty'. It's an old anthem, but it's the theme of the night.

As the music blares, there's nothing but fun to be had by all. Selfies are being snapped, dance circles are being formed, the odd drink is being spilled, and we are living our best lives. Michael is in the middle of a circle doing a tuxedo-ed shake-a-leg when MJ appears with her spectacular cleavage on offer for all to appreciate. I take it as an opportunity to sit down, and she grabs my spot on the edge of the circle to take a few more pics.

'I need some water, I'll be back, you keep dancing,' I sing out over the music to the others.

When I head back to the table, Daniel and Dusty are in deep conversation, both wearing frowns, and I hope nothing is wrong with their parents. Dusty's tie is loosened, jacket off, and his sleeves rolled up, as if it's already the end of the night and he's been on the dancefloor for hours.

'Hey, handsome, all okay?' I ask as Daniel motions that he's heading to the bathroom.

'Yep, all good. Danny Boy is heading home soon. I might leave with him?'

I'm startled. 'What? Why? Aren't you having fun?'

'Sure am.' He pauses, and I can tell he's trying to think of a reason. 'These shoes are like your old tight boots,' he squeezes my hand, 'and it was a longer drive than usual with the accident delays.'

Truth is I can see that he's tired, and I feel his pain with his shoes, but I really don't want to leave yet. Daniel returns and Dusty stands up.

'So you're definitely going, then?' I can hear the disappointment in my voice.

'You have fun. I'll dance with you later.' He winks, and I get a tingle between my legs. That's the most important dancing, anyway. He bends down and plants a kiss on my lips. I fumble for my keys and explain which one is for the screen door and which for the front door.

'I'll figure it out, Sweedard. Make sure you're home before midnight, Cinderella.'

As I watch Dusty and Daniel leave, I kick off my own shoes and take a long sip of my cab sav when MJ plonks down beside me. 'This camera is heavy when you're trying to look sexy on the dancefloor.'

'You look hot, babe, seriously hot.'

'You know who's hot?' MJ asks with a cheeky grin. 'Michael is hot.'

'Yes, he is.'

MJ looks towards the dancefloor. 'Are you sure you're okay if I have a crack?'

'Sure.' I shoo her away from the table.

Friends and peers come and go from the table, and we have fun snaps taken in the photo booth. I realise I'm a bit tipsy when I almost knock over the Pro Vice-Chancellor of the university.

*Oops.* I sit myself down and kick my shoes off again just as Michael returns to the table, sweaty from hours on the dance floor.

'Where's Dusty?' he asks, sitting down next to me.

'He and Daniel took off, tired, non-dancers. It's all good,' I assure us both. 'MJ was looking for you.'

'She found me,' he says. 'I think it might be a good time to get on the road, actually. It's nearly finished.'

He pushes his chair out and takes my arm to help me up, then clocks that I'm barefoot. He grabs my shoes and my wrap in his other hand. 'Come on, up you get. We can avoid the rush to get out and the lights coming on, because my makeup is a mess,' he jokes.

'You're wearing makeup? That's why your skin looks *so* perfect.' I run my hand over his smooth cheek and realise I'm in full close-talking-tipsy mode.

Michael chuckles. 'Okay, let's get your shoes back on.' He bends down and tries to be Prince Charming, slipping my shoes back on with some effort. I'm grateful I can lean on him as we walk down the stairs onto Queen Street. I hear MJ sing out from the entrance of Customs House.

'Bye, Annabelle, call me, Michael.'

'MJ's *very* interested in you,' I tell him.

'MJ's not the one I'm interested in,' he says.

I barely hear him as I stumble to the car and gratefully take my shoes back off.

As we drive back to Paddington, Michael puts the radio on and we both hum along to the tunes as they play.

'Did you have a good time?' I ask loudly over the music.

'I really did. I hadn't danced in a long time, and it was so good to see mob I hadn't seen for years.' We chat happily about the great company that was out on show tonight.

By the time we take the stairs from the carpark to my unit, I've graduated to feeling a bit nauseated. Michael has his right arm firmly around my waist as we take one step at a time, very slowly. The light is on above my door, which is ajar when we reach the top of the staircase.

'What a great celebration of mob excellence,' Michael says, continuing our conversation from the car. 'So proud of all those young ones living their dreams.'

'Me too. I wish Dusty had stayed till the end. He just doesn't seem to have the same passion for Black stuff like we do.'

'Different people, different life experiences and journeys, means different priorities. It's only a problem if you don't share the same values in life, Annabelle.'

'I guess you're right,' I sigh heavily and try to straighten up as much as I can. 'Thanks for the lift home, neighbour. Have a good night.'

'Night.'

As Michael walks off, I sing up the stairwell, 'Don't let the bed bugs bite.'

When I walk inside, Dusty is stretched out on the couch, TV on but volume low. I slip out of my dress, walk over, and snuggle up to him, but it's some minutes before his whole body responds. I assume he is just tired, like me. No words are spoken and the lovemaking is slow, quiet, dreamy.

The next morning, Dusty sits eating toast while I plan out my day and week ahead.

'I'll be flat out all week with meetings, and tomorrow with some media, so apologies up front if I'm slow to respond to your messages.' I'm hoping he doesn't know that I pounce on his texts with excitement as soon as they arrive each day. 'Have you got a busy week? I mean, do you have some spare time?'

'For what?' he asks.

'I was thinking that if you're going to be my hot plus one for things like this all the time, then we should probably get you another suit.' I smile, hopeful that he's been thinking about more nights out together too. 'Maybe a navy one, or a linen one in a neutral colour, and then you don't need a tie either, just a white shirt, or even a t-shirt underneath would look hot.' I start washing veggies for my meal prep later in the day. 'And if you have time for a trim, that'd be good too,' I suggest. 'I'll be getting my hair done also, and a little tidy-up for you might be worthwhile.'

I scrape the lettuce from the chopping board into a container, then turn to smile at Dusty, who holds his coffee cup up in a wordless toast to me. I blow him a kiss and start slicing tomatoes.

# CHAPTER TEN

The countdown to opening night is being calculated in days, hours, and minutes, and the staff's collective nervous energy is electrifying. I feel like I'm really leading a team in a way I haven't experienced before. The autonomy the board has given me to pull together the exhibition, and the trust and respect I have by and for my co-workers, is really turning GoFNA into a place where creatives and others will want to work, and artists from across the country will want to be exhibited in the future. My vision of being the best I can be in my field is becoming a reality.

Daniel is staying in a hotel nearby so he can easily get to the gallery each day, preferring to be there when his work is hung. I've experienced enough temperamental artists in my career to know it's easier to involve them than have them unhappy – or worse, complaining – on opening night and beyond. It's also good to have him on hand for any last minute or specific issues we need to clarify or attend to.

I do a final review of the catalogue and think that it'd be nice to sell several works on the eve of my birthday. That would be the perfect present. I've only been in the role six months, so no-one here knows it's my birthday in two days' time, and I've been so busy with the exhibition that even though the girls have tried, nothing has been coordinated to celebrate. I'm actually happy about that – I much prefer to celebrate other people's birthdays. As I sit in my office and go through the guest list, I see Dusty's name and I realise how quiet he's been since the night of the ball. I go to the office door and ask Daniel to come in for a minute.

'Good to see there's quite a few of the Davies mob coming tomorrow night, Daniel,' I say, trying to sound offhanded.

'Yeah, my family may not understand all my work, but they do support me every chance they get. I am sure all my parents' friends have my artwork in their homes. And I always go to the PBA events for the nephew because that's what family does.'

I smile. 'That's a good trade.' I can't help but mention Dusty. 'Maybe we can convince your brother to buy a piece.'

'The day Dusty buys a piece of my artwork, I'll get on a mechanical bull and ride it nude!'

'That's a bit dramatic, so let's hope it doesn't come to that,' I say with a tight smile. 'Though we do want red dots next to all these pieces.' I look out towards the walls covered in Daniel's work. 'About Dusty,' I begin, 'he's been a bit quiet since the ball. Is there something I should know? Is he okay?'

'He's fine, as far as I know. He sounded okay on the phone this morning when we discussed getting Mum and Dad here for the opening.'

'Oh, that's good. He was a bit funny at the ball and the next day, don't suppose you know why?'

'You want the truth? Or . . .'

'Well, I can tell you I don't want the "or" . . .'

He sighs, like he was expecting this exact conversation, and dreading it. 'Annie, your life is this gallery. This is in your blood, it's your number one, two, and three priorities, and that's just the start.'

'So?'

'So, within that is also your commitment to the arts generally, to social justice and human rights awareness through the arts, and your care for the creatives. And then there's your friends.'

'So?'

'*So* that's a significant list of priorities before you even get to Dusty, and without you even considering what Dusty's list of priorities looks like.'

'What are you trying to tell me?' I feel a bit under attack.

'Look, I'm asking you this as his brother – where does Dusty fit on that list, and what are your priorities in your relationship with him? And I don't mean you choosing what he wears to the beach and whether he smokes.' He pauses and considers the expression on my face. 'Yes, he told me, the night of the ball, after you left him to dance.'

'But he told me to. He literally said, "Go dance".'

Daniel shakes his head. 'That's because he didn't want to ruin your night. You like to dance, he doesn't. He wanted you to be happy, but that doesn't mean he was happy sitting like a shag on a rock till I sat with him. It was hard enough for him to suit up for the night. He was the definition of a square peg, in his mind.'

'Lots of men don't dance and the women dance together. It shouldn't have been a big deal.'

'Annabelle, I think you're missing the point. Frankly, you're being dismissive of the efforts Dusty has made for you and the sacrifices he's making for you. He's constantly out of his comfort zone to be near you. Not to pry, but what sacrifices are you making for him?'

I sink into my chair, slightly embarrassed, and a bit ashamed. I may not have made sacrifices to the same degree as Dusty, but I did compromise my values around animal cruelty to go to the PBA and the campdraft. But before I have the chance to mention this, my phone rings, putting an end to the conversation. Daniel gives me a nod and leaves, pulling the door behind him. I send the call to voicemail because I'm a bit shell-shocked and not in the mood for talking to anyone else.

\* \* \*

That night I'm running in circles trying to tidy my flat, choose an outfit for the opening, and sort out in my head what Dusty and I need to discuss. I've been replaying everything Daniel said to me, so blunt, so painfully honest, and I'm emotionally exhausted, feeling like someone has been standing on my chest all afternoon. A few tears fall. I'm not sure if they're for Dusty or not, but I recall Nanna Sony saying that no man deserves your tears, and whoever does deserve them won't make you cry.

'Knock, knock,' Michael sings out through the screen door. He hasn't done that since before the NAIDOC ball and it's comforting just knowing he's in the building. 'Just dropping this in now in case it's too hectic tomorrow night and we don't get to chat. Thought you could put it in the fridge and crack it when you get home.' He hands me a bottle of bubbly.

I give him a peck on the cheek and feel the bristle of his five o'clock shadow. 'That's so thoughtful and a great idea.' I know Dusty won't drink it, but I'll need it for sure.

He looks at the vacuum and cleaning products in the middle of the room, dresses strewn around the place, and asks, 'Do you need a hand? You look busy.'

I look at the chaos of my flat. 'You're sweet, but I'm good, thanks. But do you think we could run in the morning to clear my head before the big day? I've missed our runs.'

'Sure thing, usual time?' he asks. I nod, smile, and watch him leave. MJ told me they'd met for a drink the week after NAIDOC, but neither of them have mentioned it to me since, and I really don't want to be in the middle of it. I'm guessing there was no spark, or they did the deed and decided to stay mum about it.

Somehow, just the thought of the run with Michael has relieved me of some of the stress and anxiety of the day, and I fall into bed and sleep deeply.

\* \* \*

I spring out of bed before my alarm, full of nervous energy about the launch and about seeing Dusty again. For the first time, I'm waiting for Michael when he makes his way to the front gate.

'Well, look at you all early and chirpy. Someone's excited.' Michael's positive energy buoys me.

'I am SO excited, and I need to burn off some of this energy, so let's go!'

I take off before Michael has done his normal stretches, but he's beside me in no time, and we run at a faster pace than ever before with little chatter. With 5 km in our legs in under 30 minutes, we're both pleased with ourselves when we stop our watches.

'Wow, that was a first,' he says, wiping sweat from his brow.

'Yes, I needed to do that. Thanks. I'll see you tonight.'

'Wouldn't miss it for the world!' He flashes his toothpaste-commercial smile, and it makes me beam too.

'It's going to be amazing! I have anxiety butterflies, to be honest. I've waited so long for this moment in my career, I just hope everything goes to plan.'

'Just remember that the Gallery of First Nations Art is there for you, for us, for the world to see what we have to offer. You must believe everything will turn out as it should.' Michael's faith in what's possible is inspiring and I love that about him. As we reach my apartment, he says, 'Good luck today with the final prep and text if there's anything I can do.' He runs the next flight of stairs to his unit and the day is off to a great start.

GoFNA is empty when I walk in at 7.30 am and I use the quiet time to get some urgent emails off before the staff arrive. By 8.30, it's a hub of activity. Chairs are being placed strategically so Elders can see the speeches, tables are being set up for the drinks and glasses, and the shop is being stocked for what should be a great selling night. The baskets by local weavers from Minjerribah are already proving to be popular online with the pre-opening sale, so I make a note to speak to the artists ASAP about commissioning some more.

Daniel is there by 5 pm with a young woman, a different plus-one from the one I saw earlier in the year. This one is equally enamoured with him, doe-eyed and sticking to him like gum to a shoe.

Angel and Kev arrive early and set up the mic for her. She jumped at the opportunity to perform tonight when invited, and I love that so many more will get to enjoy her talent. MJ is weaving around the space as the official photographer, shadowed by the comms team who will go live on Insta when the official proceedings start, so that those who can't be here in person can still be part of the excitement.

CJ arrives straight from work to be part of my support crew and ease my load. Just having all my tiddas there calms me, and I'm grateful when I see them helping Elders get to their seats and fed during the night. Michael arrives solo and suited up straight from work, and comes over to give me a peck and offer to help. Between my team and my beautiful friends, everything is well under control.

As guests file through the doors, they pick up a price list and view each painting, while I make special effort with the collectors who I know will be buying tonight. When I see Mr and Mrs Davies and Naomi arrive, I head straight over to them. The greetings are brief and warm, but I'm suddenly rushed away by staff ushering me to the mic to introduce a local Elder for the Welcome to Country, then the Minister for the Arts, and Daniel. The speeches are over in record time, and I'm glad. I want the guests to have some fun, engage with and buy the art, and I want Daniel to be mingling with the collectors. And *I* want to be near Dusty, who's walked in late and hasn't had a chance to speak to me at all.

When the gallery finally empties of guests, the girls leave with some of the leftover bush tucker and I notice that Michael exits without saying goodbye, which is odd. I make a mental note to text him a thank you in the morning. I send the staff home and then I'm left with all the Davies clan as I start to close the gallery. Daniel and his family leave via the main door, but Dusty lingers, putting away the last chair. I don't know what our first words should be when he walks towards me at last.

He beats me to it, anyway. 'Congratulations, Sweedard,' he says warmly.

I lean in and kiss him. 'Thanks for your help.' I nod to the tables that he'd moved with staff when tidying up.

'All good, Sweedard. Figured the sooner we cleaned up, the sooner we could go home.' He winks and smiles and my heart melts.

'I'm parked in the side lane,' he tells me as I lock the door. When we turn the corner, I see Dusty's ute parked illegally up on the sidewalk outside the pizza place.

'Dusty! That's not even legal!'

'Let them fine me for parking on Aboriginal land,' he says.

\*\*\*

'It's after midnight,' I say as we sit slumped on the couch, my legs stretched out over Dusty's. He's running his hands absently over them in a gentle massage. 'I'm 35 but feel about 65 right now.'

'You feel about 25 to me,' Dusty says, then lifts my legs away to get up. 'I have something for you.' He goes to his bag, and I take the time to go and open the bottle of champagne that Michael dropped by. I need to toast the night, to toast me and Dusty, and my birthday.

Dusty is waiting with a small gift box when I get back.

'Is that a present for yourself?' he asks, looking at the bubbly.

'Michael gave it to me, for the exhibition.' I pour two glasses.

'He fancies you.' Dusty hands me his gift.

'No, he doesn't. He's thoughtful and generous. He's just nice.'

'I'm nice,' he whispers, kissing me hard.

'You're more than nice,' I murmur against his lips. I unwrap my gift carefully, with no hint of what's inside the tissue paper. 'Wow, a belt buckle.' *A big, blinged, belt buckle. Maybe I should have introduced him to CJ.*

'It's not just *any* buckle,' he explains. 'It's the prize I won when I was 23 years old. The night it was presented to me, I was totally overwhelmed with a sense of what I was capable of. It was the first time I really understood that I could probably make a career out of what I loved doing most, riding horses.'

'Wow!' I'm speechless at the significance of the gift.

'Sweedard, when I'm with you, I'm reminded of that moment all those years ago. And you're a woman who does what she loves. Even if I'm not that interested in art, I love that you are so passionate about it. Hell, I was even happy to be there for Danny Boy tonight. You did that, Sweedard. So I thought you deserved a prize, too.'

I move closer to him. 'This is a beautiful birthday present.'

'It's not really for your birthday, it's just for you, to have, as a reminder.'

'A reminder of what?' I ask with a frown.

'Of the fun time we've spent together.'

'Till now, but we'll have more fun times,' I say enthusiastically.

Dusty is silently looking at me and he's not smiling.

'We'll have more fun times?' It comes out as a question this time. Heat is rising up my chest into my neck and face.

'Sweedard, I can't do red carpets and balls and wear tuxedos. The beach and heights and everything you love. I don't dance and I'm not tidy and I'm not giving up smoking. The gum, I tried, but . . . none of that is me, Sweedard. That's you, It's probably Danny Boy, too. But it's not me.'

I reach out to him. 'Why didn't you just *say* something? I'm not a mind reader, so if you remain silent, then I'm left to think everything is okay.'

'Why couldn't you just *see* it? I mightn't be a smart city guy, but I know enough about you to know what you need, and want, and I know what *I* need and know where I belong and where I don't fit in.'

I open my mouth to reply, but nothing comes out.

'I'm just saying, I know you don't read minds, and I don't read books, but I *can* read what's going on here, between us.' He waves between himself and me.

That stings and I feel like I've been punched in the heart. I just want to fix it. Make us both feel happy, heard, seen, understood. All of it together.

'What do *you* need?' I ask.

'I need to not be trying to be someone or something else every minute I'm with you.'

My mouth drops. 'Every minute? You feel that way *all* the time?'

'Not when we're together in bed, but that's pretty much the only time I feel truly connected and at peace with you.'

'That's something, isn't it?'

'Of course, but we're outside the bedroom most of the time.' He goes to say more, then stops himself.

'And?' I prompt, dreading the answer.

'And I don't want to feel inadequate or a misfit *most* of the time.'

'Oh, darling, you are neither of those things.' I lunge to hug him.

'I know I'm not, but that's how I feel.' He sighs. 'You need someone more like you and I need someone more like me.'

'So you've just decided this?' It feels like he's breaking up with me but I don't want to confirm it.

He gives a complicated sort of shrug. 'I didn't decide anything, Sweedard, it just is. As much as we feel for each other, I don't fit in with your group. And I may not be as switched on as Danny Boy, but I know when people look down on me, and when they're trying extra hard to be nice to me because you asked them to.'

I sit up straight. 'What are you talking about?'

'Your friends, at Riverfire, the ball. When I say Kev was the only genuine one there, I mean he was the only one who spoke to me as me, Dusty, not as someone who's potentially wrong for you or could at least be *more right* for you. And I understand why your friends did that, I do. They're your friends and they want the best for you. And truth is, they're right. I can't say this any clearer, Sweedard. I am not right for you. And vice versa.'

I feel a pain in my heart, and it's the realisation that Dusty is smarter than I ever gave him credit for, and I've hurt him without meaning to. That truth *hurts*.

'So, what now then?' I ask.

He shrugs again.

'I know you feel something for me, or you wouldn't be here,' I continue. 'And you wouldn't have given me this.' I hold up the buckle.

'Of *course* I feel something for you. I adore you. But I don't feel comfortable in your world, and I never will.'

I take a few seconds. 'Kind of like I don't feel comfortable in *your* world. But I make it work and I have a lot of fun.'

Dusty shakes his head. 'You *make* it work. It's not meant to be *work*, not from day one, is it? Do you want to have to *make* everything work? Cos, Sweedard, I can tell you right now, I don't. I want a simple, peaceful, calm life.'

I'm deflated. I can hear the resignation in his voice, can read it in the way he's swung his legs over the side of the bed and is leaning forward, elbows on his knees.

'I'm never going to live in the city.' He looks around my flat. 'Your place is pretty, but I need a big block of land, my horses, and all my riding gear. I'm frightened of even bringing a speck of dust into your apartment.' He points to his pile of clothes strewn across my bedroom floor. 'I bought new boots just to wear to the gallery!' He nods to his boots at the door, not a scratch or speck of dust to be seen.

I'm sad and disappointed in myself, at the way I've made Dusty feel, and how I expected him to just fit in, in order for us to work, and how those expectations have led to disappointment for both of us. Rain starts falling outside. It gets heavier and heavier, and I get up to close the windows. I feel cold and sip my champagne, hoping it'll warm me and make the moment less real.

The silence hangs heavy in my bedroom.

'Dusty,' I say at last, taking his hand. 'I really am glad I met you. My world became bigger because of you, and we had some fun times. You will *always* be my cowboy.' I stroke his forearm, take a deep breath, and rip the bandaid off. 'And you're right. We should call time before either of us starts to regret what we've been to each other.'

I put the glass on the side table. 'It's late, we should get some sleep.' I slide back under the cool sheets to lie close to Dusty, willing myself not to cry, knowing this is our last night together.

'No regrets,' I say softly in his ear.

'No regrets,' he whispers back.

\* \* \*

When I arrive at the gallery the next morning, Daniel is standing in the middle of buzzing excitement and activity. I'm feeling heavy-hearted but relieved that Dusty and I have parted amicably. I take a deep breath and remember the joy in my job, especially that we need to reflect on a successful opening.

'Congratulations!' we simultaneously say to each other, and those around us cheer.

'What a night!' I give Daniel a hug. 'I think we sold most pieces. There are a couple of smaller ones left, but the big pieces are well and truly dotted with red stickers.' We high-five each other and walk into my office to debrief. It takes about half an hour before we're finished.

'Is Dusty still in town?' he asks.

'He left early this morning,' I say quietly. It's still raw. 'He gave me this.' I show him the belt buckle. 'It's my birthday, but no-one here knows.'

'HAPPY BIRTHDAY, ANNIE!' Daniel sings out so everyone in the gallery and the attached offices can hear.

The staff, already on a high from the night before, are now racing around to organise a morning tea and potential gathering after work.

'Thanks.' I smirk at Daniel.

'Dusty is a generous fella. I know he cares for you.'

'It's over,' I say bluntly.

'Ah,' he nods. 'I'm not surprised.'

'I guess I shouldn't be either.'

'He's my brother and I know him well enough to know he was always trying to please you, to be a better man for you. But he was already a good man.'

'I know that. Of course I know that.'

'And you're a good woman. You'll just both be better with other people.'

Daniel and I finalise some paperwork, then he goes to look at the paintings that sold at the opening and smiles at the number of pieces that will be going to good homes.

I spend the rest of the day thinking about my conversations with Dusty and Daniel, and how all the while I was trying to change Dusty, it could well have been me who needed changing. Maybe I need to be a little less demanding of change in other people, maybe less judgemental. I look at Dusty's belt buckle and know this will always be a reminder of him, and also of the lessons learned the last few months.

\*\*\*

At home that night, I sit on my couch, uncomfortable in my old skinny jeans, almost wishing I still had the blinged pair I'd bought especially for the campdraft. I text Michael. I want to speak to him about his quiet departure from the opening.

Hey there! Run tomorrow?

He responds instantly:

Love to but left Brissy today, sorry business, my favourite Aunt. Not sure when I'll be back. I'm responsible for almost everything as eldest nephew. Take care.

I wish I could give him a hug. I consider calling, but don't want to upset him while he's driving. I message instead:

**Here if you want to talk or need anything. XO**

I realise I miss Michael and feel bad not having had the chance to say goodbye or offer real support, but I don't know what I can do now he's left. Then Angel messages our WhatsApp group about catching up on the weekend, to celebrate my latest lap around the sun, and that's a bit of fun before I sleep.

# CHAPTER ELEVEN

It's just on dusk and the four of us are sitting under the pergola in Angel's backyard with a range of colourful and delish vegan and vegetarian dishes lining the table. With my birthday just gone and Angel's two weeks away, a double celebration is being enjoyed with caprioskas filled with fresh mint from Angel's garden, and her chickens roaming freely around the backyard.

'And another toast to the exhibition, because it was *the* best opening I have *ever* been to.' MJ is glowing in her praise as she shows us the photos she took. 'I got some great shots of you and some of your cowboy.' She winks at me.

'What's happening on the Dusty front?' Angel asks, obviously noticing that I've been quiet about him. The others lean in for the gossip.

'Dusty and I had an intense conversation when he was here. He feels he doesn't fit in my world.'

MJ blurts out, 'Because he doesn't!'

'MJ!' Angel scolds.

MJ is sober. 'Look, I'm not criticising or making fun of him. I mean, full marks for figuring that out by himself, but the man is a cowboy. A *real* cowboy. And you're here under a pergola in a Camilla Kaftan, eating hummus and drinking caprioskas and celebrating your first opening of a significant art gallery. Dusty and you? Jesus wept.'

CJ throws MJ her teacher look and Angel shakes her head.

'Be that as it may, MJ, I had feelings for Dusty,' I tell her. 'It may not have been love just yet, but I was falling for him.'

CJ slides over to my side of the table, puts her arm over my shoulder supportively, seemingly more upset than I am. 'We're here for you, Annabelle. You know that, don't you? Anything you need. We're here. You want to cry, we'll cry with you.'

'I'm fine, really. I had a little cry and I'm okay.'

MJ refills our glasses.

'I really don't think drinking more is a good idea,' I hear CJ whisper to MJ. And then to me, 'Give me your phone, please.'

'What for?'

'We're deleting his number right now.' CJ has gone from soppy supportive mode to schoolteacher mode.

'Fine! I'm over him *and* romance. It's a waste of time, and my time, like *your* time, is precious, not to be wasted.' I hand over the phone and watch as she deletes the number. I can see her looking at my text messages. 'There are none left, I deleted them all. I told you I'm okay.'

MJ is up and pacing, and I change the subject.

'What happened with you and Michael?' I ask her. 'Did you go on a date or what? He never mentioned it and has gone home for sorry business, so I didn't ask.'

'Ah Michael, yes. We went for a drink, nothing to report. There was zip going on down there,' she pauses to point to her vag, 'when I finally caught up with him.'

'Thanks for that detail,' Angel says.

'Now back to you,' MJ says, pointing at me. 'You know what you need to do?'

'Please don't say I need to go out or meet someone. Because I do *not* need to meet anyone. I didn't need to meet Dusty – that was a complete accident. If I just hadn't gone to the bar . . .' I look at Angel. 'It's all *your* fault, you know. You wanted a beer.'

'Don't blame me, I was just thirsty,' she says.

'And so were YOU!' MJ pipes in.

I laugh, like the old days, then take a deep breath. 'The truth is, I'm glad I met Dusty, even with the disappointment we weren't able to make it work. There were good times. And I learned a lot about myself, and I hope I've grown some. And,' I pause, 'I'd like a little acknowledgement for not running away from this. He started the conversation and we parted amicably.'

'Gold star for you both,' CJ says.

MJ plonks herself down next to me. 'Yeah, yeah, gold star, now focus, Annabelle. You don't need to meet someone, but you could *pretend* you're *interested* in meeting someone,' she says with a cheeky grin.

'What for?' I laugh.

'For FUN! Just post a few thirst traps on Instagram. They'll pull in the fellas, they always do, look.' MJ shows us some photos on her own Insta. 'Look, see, all those flames and hearts, all for a photo of me showing a little shoulder. Men are so fucking fickle, really,' she pauses. 'But I do like them. Look.'

She scrolls through and clicks on the profiles of some of the men who have commented on her pics. 'Him,' scrolls, 'that one,' scrolls, 'and oh, that one. Went out with *all* of them. The thirst trap really does trap them. And my vag is like the Venus fly trap.'

'My god, you are . . . I don't even have the words.' Angel is laughing but clearly shocked at this latest revelation of MJ's. 'Let me look at the caption.' Angel pushes her glasses up her nose and reads aloud. '"Coffee, tea, or me?"'

'And it looks like it was ME!' MJ raises her glass in the air in a toast to her gorgeous, sexy self.

I laugh. 'Oh my god, that is . . . it's certainly not me!'

'It's a thirst trap, Annabelle. Don't you want to prove you're okay? *More* than okay. You are *thriving!*' MJ is serious.

'I don't need to *prove* anything to *anyone*,' I assert. And I know it to be true.

CJ jumps in. 'Yes, you are thriving and shining! And you don't need to prove that to anyone. *We* see it.'

The problem is MJ is determined to post a photo of me showing some skin, in my bikini or something, with a ridiculous caption about blessing people's timelines.

I continue to say 'NO' to everything MJ proposes. I prefer my social media timelines to be full of artwork and running scenes, not me in a swimsuit.

I'm getting a headache from mixing my drinks, and MJ is still banging on about Instagram and flicking through photos of me on her own phone. 'I've got this fab photo of you on our balcony a few weeks ago. You're looking very relaxed, big sunnies, hat, a coffee, a book on the table, see?' Angel, CJ, and I lean in to look.

'I didn't even know you took that. We might need to talk about privacy,' I say, reaching for a glass of water.

MJ flaps her hands at me. 'Don't be ridiculous, this is the perfect shot. People will be wondering who you're there with. Who took the photo? A bit of mystery, bit of intrigue. And look at those long, brown legs. And we caption it, "Investing in myself". That'll attract the hot nerds, hands down.'

'You may as well do it,' Angel remarks. 'She won't let up for hours otherwise. And who knows, maybe a little bit of attention isn't a bad thing for your heart? You know I don't normally support MJ's crazy social media ideas, but maybe this once?'

'Fine,' I say, 'send me the photo and write the caption. I don't have the brain to do it right now. But I can tell you, I have faith and know the Ancestors will bring me my man when the time is right, and I'm pretty sure it won't be some random bloke on Instagram liking my photo who'll turn out to be my soulmate.'

MJ punches the air in victory and acts as if she's just won something major.

I post the photo on Instagram while we eat dinner and discuss CJ's pending teacher development day, the ethical clothing Angel wants to add to her store, and the latest romp MJ has had with a Tinder hottie from the hinterland (their meetings are all physical, apparently not a word is spoken). She won't even talk about what they *don't* talk about and we all think it's weirdly hilarious.

When I get home that night, I check my Insta out of curiosity, and I'm surprised to find Michael has liked the photo and commented 'Marambangbilang'. I'm surprised he's remembered the word.

# CHAPTER TWELVE

The sun rises brightly on Saturday morning, but I feel off-colour and unusually exhausted. I'm contemplating a walk or run, just a short trot around Paddington, hoping it will make me feel better to sweat out the indulgences of last night.

I miss Michael motivating me to get out of a morning. If he were here, we'd be pounding the pavement, up and down hills, and the endorphins would be pumping. I'd also be feeling less guilty about being so lazy since he left for sorry business weeks ago. It's strange that I haven't heard from him, though I understand that as the eldest nephew, there'd be a lot to manage his end. I bet he's exhausted, too.

I walk out onto my balcony and turn on my phone, which pings with texts and WhatsApp notifications. I scroll through and there's one from CJ:

> Just checking in, we know you're thriving, but all still okay?

Our CJ, always there for whoever needs her. I reply.

> Morning! Had a great sleep but woke up feeling blah. Probs just going to shlep around in pjs today, chill, nap, watch new season of Bridgerton. Will check in later. Have a deadly day.

I walk back inside and think about texting Michael, just to say hello and to check on him like CJ checked on me. That's what friends do. I've started drafting when my phone pings again. When I see it's Michael, I bolt upright. Talk about synchronicity!

> Hey there, how's the running going? Back home tomorrow, catch up? Or are you busy?

I respond immediately, happy he'll be back in Magandjin soon. I haven't told him about Dusty and I wonder if that's what he means about being busy.

> OMG was just thinking about you. Catch up yes, running tbd.

Michael's message is enough to get me pulling on my running gear to head outside. I feel better, lighter, happier at the thought of seeing him tomorrow. Although I'm a bit sluggish, I *am* moving, which will hopefully make it easier when Michael and I run together again. It was hard enough keeping up with him when I was running regularly.

It's 4 km from my flat to the markets at Davies Park, so I decide to run at a slow pace over the Go Between Bridge and along Maiwar. Have a coffee, grab some veggies, and walk back. The whole time, I'm thinking about catching up with Michael – hearing about his family reunion, how he managed emotionally, seeing if he needs any support.

The day passes quickly, and I watch two episodes of *Bridgerton* while ironing the week's clothes, but come nightfall, I feel off-colour again. A big bowl of steamed veggies doesn't help, so I crawl into bed early.

I wake Sunday morning with the worse period cramps since my teens. I take painkillers and cook myself a breakfast of eggs and spinach, and slump on the couch, dozing on and off.

Late afternoon comes around quickly, and I sit on my balcony with jasmine tea, still dosed up on painkillers, waiting to see Michael's car pull into the drive. I'm still in my pjs, but I know he won't just knock on my door without warning.

It's mid-September and it still cools down of a night. When the sun finally sets, I head inside for a hot shower to warm me up. I'm teary with hormones and I hope that Michael waits till the morning to catch up. No-one would want to deal with me right now.

I put the kettle on to make some more tea, and then stand under the hot running water until I feel completely warmed up. As I put clean pjs on, I start singing along to the rodeo playlist CJ put on my phone. It's become comfort listening for me somewhere along the way with Dusty. When Michael calls out over the balcony, I near jump out of my skin.

'Hey, Delta Dawn, you okay down there?' he asks with a chuckle.

'Yes, thanks! I'm sorry,' I call back, embarrassed, only half leaning over the balcony. 'I'm sure I sound like a dying cat.'

He laughs again. 'Not as bad as that.'

'Welcome home,' I say warmly, gazing up at him. He looks fresh and happy. 'It's good to have you back.'

'I'm just going to the shops, need anything? I'll pop down when I get back, okay?'

I want to say I need more tampons and painkillers but can't bring myself to ask.

'Annabelle?'

'I'm sure I've got everything I need, but thanks for asking. See you when you get back.'

'Should I wear my pyjamas too?' he jokes.

This time, *I* laugh. 'God, I've missed you,' I say out loud before I have time to think twice. I pull back from the railing.

'Not as much as I missed you, I'm sure,' he says. 'See you in about an hour.'

I sit back down and consider my impromptu declaration to him, and his response. I don't know how much time passes after Michael goes, but I feel the temp drop while sitting there trancelike, thinking about how much I actually *have* missed my generous, thoughtful, go-to-the-markets-with-me running buddy.

I'm so lost in the realisation that Michael actually did leave a gap in my life when he went home that I don't notice when his car pulls into our driveway. My playlist is still blaring and I don't immediately hear the knocking on my door until his voice comes with it. 'Annabelle!'

I straighten my pjs – I didn't even think to get dressed – and open the door. 'Welcome home!' I say again.

'Hello,' he says, walking in and giving me a hug. I hold him a second too long I think and hope he doesn't feel awkward. 'Are you okay?'

'What do you mean?' I ask, thinking he's referring to the hug. He waves his hands up and down at my pjs and general dishevelled state. 'Ah, not feeling 100 percent, that's all. Early night is needed.'

'I didn't want to say anything, but you do look like death warmed up.'

'Wow, tell me what you *really* think?' I snipe as he walks into the living room.

'I don't mean to be rude, but you need to turn that music off before someone calls the police for noise pollution.'

I think he's joking, so I don't move to stop the music.

'Where's the cowboy tonight?' Michael asks. 'Why isn't he here taking care of you, if you're not well?'

'Dusty and I broke up.'

'Oh, I'm sorry.' He pauses. 'You okay? Is that why you're feeling sick?'

I laugh. 'No. I mean yes, I'm okay, fine, good. And he's not the reason I feel sick. And I don't think it'd be fair for Dusty to have to hike down here to take care of me every month, if you get my drift.'

'Ohhh,' Michael says, understanding immediately. 'I have sisters,' he says knowingly.

'We broke up the night of the gallery opening, but you left the next day and I didn't want to bother you when you were on sorry business.'

He nods. 'But is it really over? Because, you know, people are often on again, off again.'

'Yes, it's off, not going to be on again.'

'But you really liked him. You must miss him.'

'I *did* really like him. But the reality is, as everyone knew – you, me, the girls, and Daniel apparently – Dusty and I didn't have a lot in common. He wasn't into the arts, he didn't like running, he was happy to eat in pubs all the time. And not that there's anything wrong with that, but it was just at the opposite end of the spectrum to my list of likes in life. And it turns out, I wasn't even considering *his* likes, and without realising it, I was putting in a pretty good effort to make him change himself for me. I think I liked the idea of turning the dusty cowboy into the shiny city guy. Overall, I'm surprised he hung around as long as he did.' I stop, because I don't want to be talking about Dusty when I've just realised how much I actually missed Michael these past weeks, and *he* thinks I'm missing Dusty. 'I'm sorry, I'm rambling.'

'No apologies, but you're going to have to stop feeling sorry for yourself. Secondly –'

Before he can add anything else, 'Sea of Heartbreak' comes on and he puts his hand out. 'Give it to me,' he demands.

'Excuse me?'

'Please, give me your phone. I am going to delete that godawful playlist or the entire app if I must, but either way this music is going to stop, now.' He's *not* being funny and I don't know why.

'Stop being so bloody dramatic,' I say, heading to the couch to pick up my phone.

He starts laughing. 'As if that isn't the pot calling the kettle black.'

'And what does that mean?'

'You knew that fella for how many months? And you also knew he wasn't a good fit from day one, and now you're all regretful and "sick" like he was the love of your life and he died? I don't know what transpired between the two of you and I hate seeing you upset like this, but honestly, are you surprised? Because as you say, even his brother could see it was wrong.'

I fall backwards on the lounge and frown. 'Why are you being so mean? I already said I'm not upset about Dusty.'

Michael looks at me in my pjs and shakes his head. 'I stood by for a few months and watched you, an intelligent, totally gorgeous, amazing woman, carry on like a goose over a bloke who was completely wrong for you. I wanted to tell you to snap out of it, but what right did I have?'

I'm taken aback by Michael's words.

'And now you're all sad and emotional. Please. You make me weak.'

Michael is really starting to shit me now. 'Listen to me when I say this, for the *third* time, I'm not sad, *or* emotional, I'm bloody *hormonal*!' I say through gritted teeth. 'And I'm disappointed in myself, for apparently completely lacking any self-awareness at times. But,' I stand up, 'I'm glad for the experience. I know I've grown from it.' I start walking towards the kitchen, then turn around. 'And anyway, it happened weeks ago now, it's old news. Which you'd *know*, if you bothered to contact me.'

'I'm sorry I didn't keep in touch,' he responds, annoyed.

'Oh my god, I'm *kidding*!' I say, throwing my arms in the air. We've apparently both lost our sense of humour. 'I didn't *expect* to hear from you. Your list of priorities with family would've been long, I didn't expect to even be on it at all.'

'That's the thing, Annabelle. You *are* on my list of priorities. You're at the top of it.'

I frown again. 'What?'

'I didn't contact you because I needed time to think, to assess what would happen when I came back here and you were with Dusty. Because quite frankly, I didn't think I could live in the same building anymore if you were. I was prepared to move.'

'What? Why?'

'All those mornings running, walking, talking, sharing. We got to know each other and I realised I fancied you.'

We stand facing each other, both rigid.

'And I came here tonight, and he's gone and you're not well,' he continues, 'and I just want to hold you and take care of you, because . . .' he pauses, 'because I *care* about you. Deeply.' His whole body seems to relax.

I move into him and put my arms around his neck. He holds me tightly. 'Every woman needs a man like you in their lives,' I mumble into his chest. 'You hug like a lumberjack.'

It takes a few seconds, but he says softly, 'I've never met a lumberjack, but I'll take your word for it.'

We stand silently for a few moments, then he pulls back and looks into my eyes. In that moment, something in my universe shifts. I feel it, he feels it, we both know it.

'The Ancestors came through,' I say.

'What?' He takes my hands in his. My heart begins to race and my breathing accelerates. When my stomach begins to flip-flop, I know it's because I'm here with him. I can't find any words because I'm confused by my sudden chemical reaction to the man I've never allowed myself to think about sexually, my neighbour, my friend.

Before I can finish my thought, Michael is gently guiding my chin up. My head spins as our lips meet, and I'm floating above the clouds en route to heaven. I don't know how long the kiss lasts, but when we finally break apart, my eyes remain closed.

'Annabelle?' Michael's voice drifts gently into my ears.

I open my eyes. 'What just happened?'

'We kissed.'

'I don't understand.'

'Kissing is when your lips touch someone else's,' he jokes wryly.

'But there was tongue.'

'That's when there's passion behind the kiss.' He smiles. 'Do I need to google a better definition for you?' He tucks my hair behind my ear.

'We should've done this long ago.'

'You were with Dusty.'

'And we were *friends*, and you're my neighbour, and so I never allowed myself to think of you *that* way. Did you think of me *that* way?'

'For the longest time!' he almost shouts. 'All those morning runs and walks, you know I love them, but I really like a sleep-in, too.'

I grin. 'I thought you were a fitness freak.'

'I'm only this fit because of you, because I wanted to see you, be near you, start my day with *you*. If I showed any other woman this much attention, they'd think I was flirting. But not you, *no*, you made me work so hard just to get here tonight.'

My heart swells and beats fast, and my mouth is dry, palms sweaty. The pieces to the puzzle of my heart are suddenly falling into place. 'So you don't just want to run with me in the mornings?'

'No, I'd like to sleep in with you in the mornings, too, at least a couple of times a week.' He's naughty and flirty, and I like it. His weirdness these past months makes sense to me now and I'm shaking my head at how stupid I've been, how blind to this incredible man.

'I'm sorry,' I say, taking his hand in mine.

He squeezes it. 'So now you know.'

'I am *so* glad you didn't hook up with MJ, because that would be awkward.'

'Truth is, I didn't want to go out with her at all, but she's your friend and I didn't want to offend her. We ended up talking about you the whole time, anyway. She didn't tell you?'

'No, she didn't.'

'Well, here we are,' he says, moving back to the couch.

I feel relieved, heartful, and dazed at the same time. 'You, Michael – you were right here the whole time.'

'Yes, I was.' Michael smiles and I feel immediately at peace and safe.

I shake my head and laugh. 'I can already hear the girls telling me they told me so. And there's no red dust!' I joke.

'There's not a speck of dust in any colour. Look at me!' He does a few model poses with a wink.

'Look pretty good from what I've seen so far.' I wink back. He looks damned good indeed. I lean in and kiss him gently, amazed at how this extraordinary man has seen me at my best and today, far from my best, and still wants to be with me.

'Please tell me I'm not dreaming,' I whisper, leaning in to kiss him again.

'You're not dreaming, Annabelle, and neither am I.'

# ACKNOWLEDGEMENTS

The characters in *Red Dust Running* are fictional, but I may have drawn inspiration from my rodeo-researching posse. For that, I thank my deadly tiddas who donned denim, boots and blinged belt buckles, and did road trips, sang country songs, attended rodeo, bull riding and other events, to bring this story to life.

Thank you, Naomi, Christine, Emma, Angela, Mandy, KJ, Belinda and Bec for advice, support and a sense of adventure from day one.

Thank you to the Brisbane writing and reading babes who offer endless support for all my work and me personally – Fiona Stager, Susan Johnson, Sally Piper, Mirandi Riwoe, Kris Kneen, Ash Hay, Cass Moriarty, Kris Olsson, Laura Jean McKay, Laura Elvery and Christine Jackman.

As always, I've had an incredible team at S&S, and I thank Cass Di Bello, Rosie Outred and Anna O'Grady, plus the wonderful Allanah Hunt for her copyedit.

*Red Dust Running* was originally published as an Audible Original and I thank my team on that edition: Karen Walker, Radhiah Chowdhury and Melanie Saward.

I acknowledge the support of the University of Queensland and the team at the Aboriginal and Torres Strait Islander Studies Unit, with special thanks to Robyn Donnelly, and my academic peers Prof Bronwyn Fredericks, Prof Tracy Bunda, A/Prof Katelyn Barney and A/Prof Levon Blue.

I researched and wrote this novel on the lands of the Jagera, Turrbul, Bidjigal, Darrumbal and Githabul peoples, and I acknowledge and respect their Ancestors as the original storytellers of those lands.

Read on for an excerpt from
*Not Meeting Mr Right* by Anita Heiss

Available in paperback, ebook and audio

# 1

# I love being single

'I love being single!' I said, with such conviction I almost believed it myself. All of a sudden I was desperately trying to convince myself and the table of proud married mothers that I really, really loved my single life just the way it was, and had no desire to marry and/or breed, thank you very much. Until I'd arrived at the pub that night, it had pretty much been true.

It was two months after my twenty-eighth birthday and I was at my ten-year school reunion at the Hub in Bondi Junction, our stomping ground in our late teens. Back then it had been known as Jack's Bar. I'd dreaded the night since the invitation had arrived and had spent the previous three months mentally scripting and planning the event. It was sure to be an unpleasant reminder of what school had been like. I'd been a self-conscious teenager who never really fit in – me being a Blackfella from La Perouse and the rest of the girls whitefellas from Vaucluse and Rose Bay.

A triangular peg in a round hole, I used to say. I'd never felt skinny enough or pretty enough compared with the other girls.

I wouldn't even have gone, if Dannie hadn't almost physically dragged me along. I'd much rather have stayed away – or boycotted, as Bianca had put it. Bianca had better things to do, like 'hanging out with her man', she'd said. The three of us had remained friends after school, but Dannie was married now, Bianca had just got engaged, and me, well I was *loving being single*. We seemed an unlikely trio, but somehow we were mates.

I was now the head of the history department at a private Catholic girls school, living in a cool one-bedroom apartment full of sunlight at Coogee Beach, and I'd aged well compared to my old school buddies. I'd thought that would be more than enough to see me through the reunion with head held high, but within minutes of ordering my first gin and tonic, it was clear that my old classmates weren't impressed. In their eyes, I was without the one key ingredient that determined success and true happiness: I did not have my Mr Right. I was the only one at the table who didn't, but they made me feel like I was the only one on the planet. This time I was prettier and thinner than most, but they had all moved on. They had all joined the 'club' – the 'I have a significant other and significant little others' club.

The reunion was set up like a speed-dating event. Everyone was allocated a specific amount of time speaking to the person opposite them; when the time was up, one side of the table moved left to face someone new. The idea was to keep on doing this until everyone had the chance to catch up with everyone else. The conversations so far, though, had all been about wedding planners, floral arrangements, dress fittings, honeymoon locations and gift registries. I'd never had a bridal register, or a wedding planner, and with no similar experiences of my own to share or compare, I felt left out.

Now I sat opposite Estelle and just listened, sucking on the ice from the bottom of my first drink.

'Excuse me, Alice,' she said as she rearranged her rather bulky bra, 'My nipples are killing me.'

'What!' I spat ice back into my glass. Was there a new dinner-table etiquette I was unaware of that meant it was okay to discuss sore nipples in public?

'Still breastfeeding and my son just *tugs* on them.'

She put her whole hand in her bra.

'Really . . .' I didn't know what else to say, but it didn't matter. She continued right on.

'At least the pain isn't long term – not like stretch marks or the need to do pelvic floor exercises every day.' Estelle grimaced and I guessed she was tightening her vag. It wasn't a good look. Right at that moment I seriously loved being single: sore nipples, loose vaginas and stretch marks didn't appeal to me at all.

I was bored already, and food wasn't even in sight. I eavesdropped briefly on the conversation next to us.

'I registered at Peter's of Kensington – they do the best bridal baskets,' I heard Louise say.

'I was with DJs, but seeing as it was my second wedding, I wanted to keep it low key,' Judi responded. I couldn't believe these women were actually for real.

*I love being single!* had been my daily mantra for the last couple of years. Serial dating and short-term relationships suited me fine. My single life was great compared with the lives of some married women I knew. God knows the teachers at school who had kids always looked tired and were on the run all the time.

No-one I'd spoken to so far had seemed convinced by my *I love being single!* mantra, though. They'd responded only with 'Of course you do!' and 'There's absolutely nothing wrong with being single.' But to me they sounded condescending and that got my back up. Within the first half-hour, all my insecurities about not being skinny or pretty compared to the other girls in the school grounds had come flooding back.

I should have taken note of my horoscope that morning: 'Expect the unexpected! Remember your own value.' Let's face it, while I hadn't expected to have a raging good time at the reunion, I sure as hell hadn't expected to be tripping over my self-esteem because of it either. Aria's Super Stars were nearly always right when it came to Leo predictions and I always, *always* relied on her words of wisdom to see me through the day, but today they weren't providing me with enough positive affirmation to deal with the reunion.

Someone gave me the shove to move left again. I didn't know whose idea the speed dating set-up was, but it was genius. I moved on, leaving Estelle's sore nipples for someone else to soothe.

'*I love being single!*' I said to Linda, before she had the chance to talk about any part of her anatomy or any special exercise regime she might be following. I looked down at my cleavage. 'And my nipples are fine.' I thought I'd get in first. 'No stretch marks, and I haven't been too stretched downstairs either!' I laughed.

Linda looked at me oddly, and asked, 'How many kids have you got, Alice?'

'None. I'm a bleeder, not a breeder,' I said, half trying to be funny, half serious. Linda just smiled politely and showed me a couple of photos of her children. Admittedly, they were cute, but when she put her phone back down on the table, we looked at each other blankly. I hadn't ever really thought about kids, not seriously. Not seriously enough to have a meaningful conversation with a mother about parenting, anyway.

Of course I'd dreamt about meeting Prince Charming and having a fairytale wedding. Most girls do. I'd started planning my wedding when I was only twelve and we'd had a mock ceremony in the street where I grew up. Richard Barker played the groom. He wore a school tie with his shorts and t-shirt and I wore a pink dress and a shower curtain on my head as a veil. Since then I hadn't become Muriel by any means, but I had bought the odd wedding magazine over the years, just to look at the pictures, and I'd been to one or two bridal fairs. All women did, didn't they? I called it research. I was a teacher; I liked to be organised. No-one wants to be running around at the last minute once the question has finally been asked. Yes, even single girls have bridal dreams occasionally. Women who say they've never thought about a fancy wedding are lying. Problem was I'd not given any thought to what would happen *after* the wedding. All I really wanted was a man. A wedding would be fun too. But married life? Not for me.

I was glad to get the nod from Jen, the class bossy-boots, to move on. 'I think our time's up, Linda. Pity . . .' We both half smiled. Even if I only had to spend a short time speaking to every woman there, it was still going to be a struggle. I was beginning to feel inadequate: I was an intelligent, educated, capable woman, unable to make conversation, even basic small talk, with girls I'd spent six years at school with. Why didn't we have anything to talk about?

Don't get me wrong. It wasn't as though I wanted to talk about current affairs all night – refugees, Indigenous health, peace in the Middle East – but *some* diversity would've been appreciated. Talking to Jen would be a welcome break. I'd loved having her in my Society and Culture class in senior years – she always brought something quirky to every discussion.

'So Alice, I've been looking forward to speaking to you. You were always so political at school. I've just joined this new party, and I thought you might be interested in it.' Thank god – Jen hadn't changed at all. 'Cool, which party? What's its platform?' I was already feeling more comfortable. Politics were a level playing field. Didn't need kids to be political.

'It's the Family Party – we advocate for protecting traditional family values; the family is the most important thing.' She rattled this off as though she was reciting the party line.

I nearly dropped my drink. Was I sitting with a mobster's wife, a Scott Morrison fan, or just a lunatic?

'So, what does the party think of same-sex marriages?' I asked, baiting her.

'They don't endorse anything that's not in the Bible.'

'Female clergy, then – you always believed in equality for women in society.'

'No, there are definite roles for men and women, and the clergy isn't for both sexes.'

'Abortion?' I could tell I'd hit a nerve as Jen started to fidget. Her politics were bad politics, but she wasn't an idiot. I'd thought if I made her say the words out loud she might see how ridiculous her position was, but she didn't respond at all. She knew I knew the answer to this question already. It seemed even the political conversations tonight would be hijacked by notions of motherhood and womanhood and narrow definitions of family.

'The party does support a Voice to Parliament Alice,' Jen said almost proudly. 'You'd appreciate that. I saw your insta reel about the referendum last week.'

So the party had *one* decent item on their agenda – their support for Blackfellas didn't discount the fact that they were homophobic and sexist. Who'd want to work alongside that mob anyway? None of my friends would.

'Why exactly did you join this party, Jen? You seemed so broad-minded at school.' I was blunt.

'Because my husband did, and I support his views. That's what married life is about. Support and compromise.'

My stomach turned. Not only had Jen taken on extreme right-wing political beliefs, but she hadn't even thought them through for herself. Or had she? Did she truly believe she had to adopt her husband's views? If I married a guy whose political beliefs didn't match mine – highly unlikely – *I* sure as hell wouldn't be crossing the floor in the name of wedlock. I had to do a reality check. Was it 1950? Was I actually at Jack's Bar listening to this? Had we all been taught the same things at school? If so, what had gone wrong? Was it me? Surely not!

I looked around the table for some answers and all I saw was a group of women who had lost their own sense of identity. They were all now known as Mrs Joe Bloggs or Mrs Sue Jones-Bloggs or Emily Bloggs's mother. But they all seemed happy. Why was I so angry? Was it possible I was feeling envy?

As luck would have it, I was opposite Dannie next, and our entrees arrived, so I had some respite from trying to fit in. It was an opportunity to bone up on some birthing detail, too, before I had to move left again.

'So, how many waters are there anyway?' I whispered. 'And what do you do if they break on a bus?' Dannie – my only married friend – thought I was joking, but in all honesty, I had no idea what my old classmates had been talking about. Why would I? There's an unrealistic expectation that every woman is maternal and is born to breed. Not me. I wasn't maternal at all.

'Seriously, Dannie, does meeting Mr Right and breeding with him mean that women can't think or talk of anything else from that moment on?'

Dannie wasn't offended, she just laughed and changed the subject. 'What did you think of *The Daily Terror*'s report on the Black Lives Matter Movement last Saturday, Alice? I've been waiting all week to hear your opinion.'

Dannie was the least wife-and-mother-like married woman I knew – partly because she hung out with me so much. She was doing a media degree part-time at uni, so we had common interests still. Dannie recently wrote a paper about the death of Queen Elizabeth and she had bit of a rant about it now:

'We can't get any recognition or accountability for Black Deaths in Custody. We can't get a public holiday for a Day of Mourning, but we *can* get a public holiday when the colonising Queen dies AND parliament also stops for 15 days of mourning? Please, could the government be any more offensive, or insensitive?' Dannie was a staunch republican. I loved her even more for that.

She hadn't been sucked into any void of wifedom and motherdom; she was on top of the rest of life's responsibilities as well. The other women at the table could have learned a lot from Dannie.

After we'd finished our entrees, we moved on again. Vicky was across from me now. She was considered to be promiscuous back when we were at school, because she spent so much time up the Bronte gully with boys from the surf club. The gully was far behind her, though: she had gone on to become a highly paid lawyer with one perfect child and a second husband who was a well-known QC.

She specialised in corporate law and didn't do any pro bono work at all. (I asked.) She couldn't really afford to, she told me, with childcare fees and a huge mortgage on their Point Piper home.

'There's such a limited number of childcare places in this state that some of us have to pay double just to find someone to mind the kids.' Vicky made it sound as though raising her own child was an imposition. It was an attitude that always made me angry.

I'd been waiting weeks to have this conversation, after listening to whining mothers on talkback radio and I launched straight in. 'I don't understand women complaining about the government not providing enough day care centres.'

'Women have to work too.' Vicky sipped her wine. 'Have to or *want* to? You wouldn't *have* to work if you lived somewhere other than Point Piper, surely.' There was no way she was getting away with not admitting it was her lifestyle that meant she *had* to work.

'We're part of society – why shouldn't we be out there in it every day?'

In my mind, there was a difference between participating in society and dumping your kids with a stranger so you could make money.

'If *you* choose to bring a child into the world, *you* should be responsible for raising it. Feeding it, playing with it, looking after it until the child goes to school.'

'What's your real problem with working mothers, Alice?' Vicky asked. It sounded like a challenge, as if the issue was really about me, and not about working mothers.

'I don't have a problem with mothers working. I just don't understand how parents can admit publicly that they're pissed off they can't find a stranger to raise their children for $100 a day. Aren't kids supposed to be your most prized possessions? Or are some things more important than children? I wouldn't be off-loading my little one to some stranger to raise, just because I wanted a big house in an expensive suburb.'

'Ah, but you're single and childless, Alice, it's different for you.'

'That's right – it should be different for me! I am single and childless, so I can work long hours without it affecting anyone else. I can be – what would you call it? Selfish?' I was getting hot, my face felt flushed.

Vicky remained cool. She wasn't buying into the argument. Her kid was probably in some private centre that cost a fortune anyway. Vicky would've had a cleaner and probably a cook, dog-walker, social director and third husband on the way. She clearly had more than me – even though as a single woman I was socially permitted to be *selfish*.

We'd reached a stalemate – but our time was up.

Neither of us bothered with a polite smile; I just stood up and moved one seat to the left again.

I persevered with the reunion chatter for quite some time, fighting hard to find new adjectives to describe each family portrait and baby photo I was forced to look at over the course of the next hour. I tried to expect the unexpected, as Aria had advised, hoping that among all these women, there might be a Toni-Morrison-reading, Koori-Radio-listening, Villawood-visiting mother who perhaps sent her kids to a Steiner school or something, and taught ESL to refugees once a week. Anything was possible, wasn't it? I mean, that's the mother I knew *I'd* be.

Eventually I found myself opposite Ronelle. She was the one person I'd been looking forward to speaking with. Teased for being overweight at school, she was now the most glamorous woman at the table. Softly spoken and relaxed, she told me she had three kids, but didn't mention stretch marks or lack of sleep or sore nipples or the need for more day care centres. Instead, she talked about her life as a yoga instructor – she'd been to India, done a course, changed her name to something like 'Swami' (I'd forgotten it five minutes later). It was all going well until she asked if I'd like to attend one of her classes 'even though they are for new mums'.

'You might still get something out of it,' Ronelle said with one eyebrow raised. 'Your bust would look better if you sat straighter, and yoga is fabulous for posture. You'd learn to relax at the same time, too.' So she thought that I *needed* yoga – that I had a drooping bust line and that I was uptight? My bust was fine, and I wasn't uptight, just annoyed at the lack of interesting conversation so far that evening. I didn't need yoga – I just didn't need to be at the reunion.

'I have too short a concentration span to make yoga work for me, Ronelle, but thanks,' I said, and moved on even though our time wasn't up, demonstrating that what I said was true.

After making a monumental effort to adhere to the rotational rule, having spoken to almost everyone, I took a break, leaning back in my chair. The metal was cold on my skin. I looked around the pub. Jack's had been gentrified, like all the pubs in the eastern suburbs had been in the past decade. Dark wood tables and comfy cushioned lounges had been replaced by streamlined chrome tables and chairs. The antique-looking carpet you still find in old people's houses had been replaced with ceramic tiles. The pokie room was now a dimly lit cocktail bar.

The space wasn't as warm as it had been when we were young, and while the pub's owners had changed its name, and spent millions updating the interiors, they hadn't really managed to change their clientele. I scanned the room and saw some of the same private-school rugby players who'd been drinking there a decade before. They didn't seem as attractive now. Funny that, everyone's a ten when they're young.

That thought brought me back to our group. There had been more of us back then, when we were teenagers. I looked around and counted heads: we were a table of thirty. Why had only fifteen showed up? Probably because the others were single and out having a raging time meeting gorgeous men, not worrying about their pelvic floors.

Then I noticed it: each and every woman in the group wore an engagement and/or wedding ring. That's why I was on the outer. That's why I didn't fit in. It was a clear case of 'Us' and 'Them'. I couldn't even pull the race card this time; it wasn't about being Black and white. It wasn't about being rich or poor, as it had been at school. Rather, at twenty-eight it was about the haves and the have-nots. I was definitely a have-not. No wedding ring – not even an engagement ring. No husband. No kids. Not even a date lined up any time in the near future. I had nothing to contribute to this Mothers' Club meeting. No-one was the slightest bit interested in what I did for a living, what I drove (unless it was the latest station-wagon or oversized four-wheel drive with airbags to protect the kids), or where I lived (unless it was near a good day care centre).

Debra, who had once crushed biscuits in my hair at the school bus stop, arrived late. She hadn't changed a bit. Thin frame, thick hair, bushy black eyebrows, and a sense of self that had always put me on edge. Where did she get that confidence? I knew straight away she'd be married with children. I really didn't care if I spoke to her or not, but she planted herself opposite me just as the main course was being served, everyone else quickly moving to ensure there wasn't a spare seat across from them. Debra was known as the mean girl at school, but no-one was ever brave enough to challenge her. Dannie had told me that no-one really wanted her to come. I'd had five gins and two glasses of wine by this time, though, so I was ready for whatever she dished out. Biscuits or otherwise.

'So, how many children do you have, Alice?' Debra had four.

'None. But here's a photo of my brothers.' Did it sound as weird as I thought it did? Probably. I quickly put my phone away and didn't show anybody else the photo that night. Some may have thought it was sad, but my brothers and my dad had always been the most important men in my life. At least I could rely on them to be there for me.

'But you're obviously involved with someone special, though,' Debra said, looking at my hands.

'No. I bought this ring as a present for myself.' I was proud of my ability to teach, and that I made a good enough living to take myself shopping at Tiffany's. If I were ever to get a wedding ring or even just an engagement ring, it would have to come in a pale blue box. Not some chain-store faux suede one.

'That's funny. I thought Aboriginal women had children young – married or not. We all thought at school you'd be the first to have children.' Bitch! Had they all really thought that?

Debra was wrong about me being the first pregnant, but she was right about Koori women and kids generally. Fact was, most of the Koori women I knew had squeezed their kids out in their early twenties, some even before that, and none of them had blokes around now. Some of them had never had a bloke around at all. Many of the young girls I knew now were still doing it. It was a hard thing for me to understand, coming from a two-parent family and a Catholic background. We'd always been taught no sex before marriage and no kids out of wedlock. Even as times changed, the morals of the Church were upheld, at least in the Aigner house. Christian values worked for me in a very general sense – do unto others and so on – but

I'd had to work out my own beliefs when I left school and started to live the life I thought best for me and the world. I tried to live by the Aboriginal value systems of the past – community benefits over individual gain, cooperation over competition, responsibility over rights.

Debra was still staring at me.

'Some do have children young, Debra, and so do many young white women in a certain demographic.' She looked at me, unbelieving. I was struggling; she'd dealt me a low blow and I didn't really know how to recover.

'As for me, I've got plenty of love around me. And plenty of work to do. I'm not looking to fill any gaps yet,' I said, getting to my feet, loud enough for some of the other women to look at me and then Debra, wondering what had sparked the clear disagreement. Debra looked at me with contempt. She was ticked off, but I didn't care.

I already had my mother nagging me about breeding and maintaining the race. ('Wouldn't it be lovely to have a little brown Koori kid around the house?') All the other women in her ceramics class had photos of their grandchildren. ('I just need one photo in my phone, Alice.') She said she was the only Koori woman without grandkids. ('It's our job as the matriarchs to have families, Alice.') Now whitefellas I didn't even like were on my case about it too.

Dessert was being served and I moved four seats away, so I could sit alone. Half the table, the 'responsible homemakers and mothers', were outside, irresponsibly sucking on cigarettes or vaping. Yeah, get lung cancer and who'll look after your man and kids then? Dannie was happily engrossed in conversation with two other women and looking like she was having a great time.

I repeated my mantra, *I love being single!*, over and over.

By ten pm, *I love being single!* had become *I hate school reunions*. The more I drank the more difficult it became.

'Here's one of Lulu as a princess and Davey as an elf – aren't they cute?' Another phone screen was shoved in my face.

I looked around the table at all the women, now totally sloshed. It was their one big night out and they were going to make the most of being kid-and husband-free for a night. It was funny that I'd been at all worried about what to wear to the reunion. My 'competition' hadn't worried at all. They might have been happy with husbands and children and shared mortgages, family holidays and family rooms, but they also bore a few more worry lines than I did, and more greys on the temples, but then I knew my spare cash went on addressing those things, not school excursions and the like. These minor details at least brought me momentary comfort. It always bothered me to see women in bicycle shorts, t-shirts and thongs out shopping, though I realised that mothers had more important things to worry about than coordinating outfits. It was okay to look sporty or beachy, I thought, but not both at the same time, and regardless of priorities and income, COVID had made it acceptable to wear activewear everywhere, but I still would never leave the house without a bra and lipstick. It was like going to work without cleaning your teeth.

'You haven't changed at all, Alice.' At last some positive recognition! It was Leonie. We had been good friends in Year 8 but then drifted apart. I faked a modest smile.

'Thanks, it's the eye cream and derma peels,' I said, trying desperately to make my existence as a single woman with a disposable income sound a little less pathetic and perhaps even indulgent. If I could make my life sound like an attractive option to just one of these women I would be happy.

'You never got that chipped tooth fixed, did you?'

I gasped. My god, she wasn't complimenting me at all.

'Not that you needed to. It's like a signature look for you.' I rarely even thought about the tiny chip on my front tooth. It had happened in year 2. I was laughing so hard I hit my mouth on a chair. I usually have to point it out to people, it's so *not* there. I was so pissed off that I felt like chipping *her* tooth, the married, mortgaged, motherly bitch!

Dannie could see I was distressed, having difficulty just being there, let alone having a good time. She handed me a glass of water.

'Why did you come?' she whispered sympathetically.

'You dragged me here, remember? You didn't want to come on your own.'

'Oh, come on, Alice. You've never done anything you didn't want to in your life. You can't blame me. Why did you *really* come?'

'Because if I didn't, people would've talked about me.'

'Don't be ridiculous.' She was right. They wouldn't have talked about me. They hadn't been talking about anyone else. They were lovely women, and genuinely keen to catch up and share baby photos and birthing tales, because that's what normal women our age did.

'I'm not normal!' I said.

Suddenly I wanted my own special moments to share: the moment when I 'just knew'. When I'd met 'the one'. The wonderful roller-coaster ride from wedding planning to broken waters.

I felt a growing desire to fit in with this group, this new community I'd never been part of. I was part of the Koori community, my local community in Coogee, and the school community (as a teacher, of course, not a parent) – but I'd never been a member of the 'married with children community'. Now I wanted in.

I wanted more than that, though. I wanted to prove it was possible to maintain your identity and keep up to date with current affairs even while changing nappies and doing canteen. I knew I could manage it. I wouldn't be like *them*. I was up to the challenge.

A man, marriage, career, kids and happiness: I *could* have it all, I decided. I *would* have it all.

'I'm going to get married,' I blurted.

Dannie shook her head. 'Listen, you're just pissed, Alice. You love being single. You're always big-noting about how good you've got it. A husband and kids? That's not for you.'

She didn't understand my resolve: I was already excited about the new path my life was going to take – until I was momentarily side-tracked by another conversation about pregnancy.

'I just loved the feeling of Sky and Fern as babies inside me,' someone said, and another round of discussion began, not about the appalling choice of names (there's a conversation I could've participated in), but about what it felt like to have a parasite *moving* inside you. Shouldn't those kinds of things be kept private? Did these women have no sense of decorum? Obviously not. I tried to imagine what they were describing, but the only thing moving in my gut was the baby octopus I'd had for dinner, and if my waters were to break now they'd have a very high alcohol content.

I started to feel sick. It wasn't just the conversation: the G&Ts weren't mixing well with the huge slice of tiramisu I'd eaten for dessert. I got up to go to the loo. Dannie jumped up too and raced towards the door, pushing past me on the way.

'I'm busting. Haven't had a chance to escape all night,' she said. Did that mean she was over it as well?

As we both sat in adjacent cubicles, I reminisced a little about the nights we used to spend as teenagers with fake IDs, hiding in the toilets until the police raid was over outside. I recognised the old tiles and wooden doors and wondered why the ladies were the only part of the pub that hadn't been brought into the twenty-first century.

'There's no paper,' Dannie said, sticking her hand under the dividing wall.

'Want to leave?' I asked as I passed her some paper.

'Why? It's only early.' Of course, this was a big night out for Dannie too; her husband George was minding the kids for the first time in months.

'Because this is soooooo painful. I don't fit in. I'm not even a bloody peg, regardless of shape. I want to go home.' I actually wanted to do a thorough post-mortem of the evening and decide once and for all – by morning, if that were at all possible – whether I wanted a man and a kid or not.

'We need to speak to everyone at least briefly.' Dannie was happy to leave with me early, but she would never be impolite, not even for her mate. We both stood at the sink washing our hands.

'I haven't spoken to Karly yet,' I said. 'At least she might be good for a laugh.' I was trying to be positive, as Dannie hadn't bitched about anyone all night.

'I haven't spoken to her either – why don't we do it together? That way it will be only *half* as painful for you.' Dannie was trying to point out how unreasonable I was being, but I just said 'Ha! Ha!' and pushed her out the toilet door.

Dannie took a seat on Karly's left and I sat opposite them. Karly had always seemed as if she was away with the pixies in class. Since school she'd been to East Timor, set up a communication network, met a missionary, and adopted three kids.

'So you're a full-time mother, then?' Dannie was more interested than I was in the motherhood side of things.

I wanted to hear about the 'missionary work' and saving souls.

'Yes. These children need all the love they can get. Poor things, it's very hard raising them outside of their own culture and society.' Karly had that martyr sparkle in her eye. I saw it. Dannie saw me see it. I saw Dannie start to move.

'Well then why are you doing it?' I asked Karly aggressively. Dannie stood up and grabbed her things.

'I thought I might call Bianca and let her know what a great time we're having. Maybe I can persuade her to come down. Why don't you come with me and say hello, Alice?' It was an escape plan; we could finally leave. I didn't care about Crusading Karly if it meant I could get out of there.

'Great idea. I'm sure she's wishing she were here,' I said, holding up my hand and mouthing a lie at Karly: 'Five minutes!'

Dannie and I linked arms and giggled as we headed towards the door.

# 2

# Strategic planning

Once outside, Dannie called home to check on her kids, and I called our friends Peta and Liza. 'I'm getting married!' I explained, and told them to meet us at my place immediately – I needed their help. They were a little worried, they both admitted later, so they agreed to meet me at mine in half an hour.

Dannie was sober enough to enjoy the opportunity to drive my sporty red VW to my place. She'd sold her Land Rover when she moved to Paddington; the street was simply too small for it.

Within the hour, the four of us were sitting around my lounge room. The globe had blown, and I hadn't replaced it, so I lit some candles. Dannie and Liza sat on the retro red sofa they had all helped me choose, and Peta and I sat on cushions on the wooden floor. It was a balmy night, so we opened the windows and venetian blinds wide to allow as much breeze in as possible. Just being home, I felt more secure in myself; I was in my own space, with my friends; two of them were happily single, childless women. In their company, I was normal, one of the majority.

'So how was the reunion?' Liza asked.

'It felt like all married women can talk about is honeymoons, anniversaries, pregnancies, Lamaze classes, sore nipples, breast milk, stretch marks, school fees, nits, mortgage repayments—' I took a breath, '*Apparently*, all the *important* things in life. Important to whom, I ask you?'

'Important to those women, Alice. Don't be so bloody harsh – or are you jealous?' Dannie was defensive. I *was* being harsh and, truth be told, I was perhaps a little jealous, but even though I admitted quietly to myself that all the women at the reunion were happy, and none of them looked like they'd trade their lives for quids, I would never let my insecurities be known publicly. Not Alice Aigner.

'Jealous, hah! I love my life. I could *build* on it, of course. In fact, I'll get myself a man, and breed, and show that it's possible to maintain a marriage, motherhood, and a mind of my own. Yep, I'll have it all by the time I'm thirty. I'll marry the most gorgeous man on the planet, have a HUGE wedding, so big it'll end up not only in the social pages of the *Koori Mail* but in the daily papers, too. You girls will be there, of course: Liza, the wedding coordinator; Peta, the producer; and Dannie, the matron of honour.'

'Why can't *I* be matron of honour?' Peta jokingly whined to Dannie.

'You're not married, and if you were, you'd be matron of *dis*honour,' Dannie said with a smile. Peta and Dannie occasionally sniped at each other, because they were so different – Peta out partying every night, Dannie relishing reading to her kids before tucking them into bed – but their exchanges were nearly always in good humour.

'Can I finish?' I felt we were losing focus. 'The difference is *I* won't be limited to conversations about cradle crap, booster shits or nappy thrush.' The girls keeled over laughing, but I had no idea why.

'Cradle *cap*,' Dannie chuckled.

'Booster *shots*,' Liza added.

'And it's nappy *rash*, Alice. Even I know that.' Peta rolled her eyes.

'Whatever! So now there's a whole language I need to learn as well. I can do that. I'm a bloody history teacher. I could learn the whole history of birthing techniques and baby things if I really wanted to. But I don't.'

Liza and Peta smirked at my outburst, but I think Dannie was a little bothered about how I pictured her as a mother. She frowned out the window into the black night, elbow resting on the arm of the lounge, her chin cupped in her palm. I wasn't talking about her at all – she had to understand that.

'Dannie, you know I don't think of you as *really* married or *really* motherly at all, don't you?'

'I don't think of you as *really* Aboriginal either.'

It was the first real laugh I'd had all night. Dannie wasn't just our voice of reason; she often provided the comedy for the group, too.

'So, you're going to be married by your thirtieth, are you, love?' Liza was good at getting things back on track.

'That's right. I've got two years. I want what all those other women have, like Dannie. I can do it, I know I can.'

'Do what? Learn how to function without sleep?' Dannie was always pragmatic.

'No, I like my eight hours' sleep per night.'

'So, you want to be able to read only when you go to the toilet, and even then have someone banging on the door calling out *Muuuuum* – your only name?'

'No, I like to be left in peace on the loo, and to read at night in bed – and on the beach too.'

'Ah, the beach. Well, be prepared to spend hours packing bags with towels, buckets, spades, cordial, sandwiches, tiny packets of chips, spare clothes and sunscreen. And don't think for a minute you'll ever be able to lie down and read anything, because you'll have to be watching the kids the whole time.'

'Okay, so forget the kids and reading for now, what about Mr Right? You have him. Tell me about how wonderful that is – having a gorgeous man who has vowed to adore you forever – your own Mr Right!'

'I have Mr All-Right. When the kids come along, it all changes between you and your man, Alice. There's hardly any more romance. George and I don't even kiss properly anymore unless we're having sex.'

'But there you have it! You *have* sex! On tap! Right?'

'We fall into bed every night exhausted, look at each

other and smile, then agree to wait until we have more energy – which of course we rarely have.'

Personally, I thought having sex with a bloke called George would be difficult at any time, but I pursued my line of questioning.

'What about the mansion? The freshly cut lawns? The young, built husband washing the car on Sunday morning, your kids riding bikes and getting good school reports, the dog you take for walks?'

'The so-called mansion takes hours to clean and keep tidy because the kids leave everything, including their bikes, everywhere. Jeremy looks like he'll have to repeat kindergarten – kindergarten! Sarah's one of the school bullies, so naturally I'm proud of her. We pay a fortune for a gardener who is so old I'd rather he *didn't* take his shirt off. George's sixpack has turned into a slab. The car is always dirty because George won't use a bucket to wash it and is too tight to pay to get it cleaned, and the fucken dog is a Siberian husky and should be in Siberia. It moults fur all over the place and eats more than me and the kids put together.' Dannie stopped and took a long sip on her drink. 'Sorry for swearing.' There was sweat on her forehead.

'Okay, okay, I get it. It's not *all* rosy, but I want *some* of it. I'll trade the kids off for a trip to Venice or Paris or anywhere each year. At least say you'll help me find a bloke. Based on what you've told me, without the kids we'll at least have the energy for sex.'

Liza jumped in. 'What you need is a strategy.' She pulled out a steno pad from her bag. Her preparedness comes from being a lawyer, always making case notes. Liza works for the Aboriginal Legal Service in the city. She's white like Dannie, but with Italian heritage. I call them my token white friends; I reckon everyone should have at least one or two. It's politically correct.

Liza and I met at a justice forum about eight years ago and have been tight ever since. Liza's really smart, she always has her head in a book, and it's always non-fiction. She has a real thirst for learning. I like her because she's genuine. Her work at the ALS isn't some patronising attempt to help Blackfellas, and it's not about making herself feel warm and fuzzy about being in the cause either. Some might see it as her bit for reconciliation, but Liza has a holistic approach. Her philosophy is that helping anyone in any way makes the world generally a better place to live. I love that about her. Also, I think she enjoys pissing her parents off. They're well-known solicitors. They wanted her to join the family firm, and hate that she works at the ALS for next to nothing. She does heaps of pro bono work as well, which her parents simply don't understand. They didn't support her attending the Black Lives Matter protests following George Floyd's death, and she didn't speak to them for months afterwards. She is so passionate about social justice that she has culled almost everyone from her life who doesn't think like she does. She can be extreme, but that's what I like about her.

Once we were in a restaurant when another member of our group – a friend of a friend – kept putting on a racist Indian accent. Liza was furious; she threw money into the middle of the table and stormed out, shouting, 'I only want to surround myself with people who think like I do!' She was accused of being narrow-minded, but I agreed totally with her, and followed her out. That was when we became close.

Peta, Dannie and I watched Liza tear off pages from her notepad and lay them on the table. Then she pulled pens from her bag. I imagine this is what she does as part of preparing for a case, but I can't be sure, because I've never really seen her in action. Unlike most of my girlfriends, Liza is all for confidentiality. If she learns something at work that she thinks I really should be on top of or might just be interested in knowing, she'll tell me, 'What I'm hearing out there is . . .' or 'The word on the street is . . .', but she never gives away anything she shouldn't. She's a good confidant, which is why I felt safe pouring out all my business in her presence. I knew she'd take it to the grave. She better.

'Okay, so let's be clear about your goal first.' Liza was methodical, too. 'What exactly is it?'

'Haven't you been listening? I want to meet Mr Right and get married *and* I want to have a HUGE, all-star-cast, social-event-of-the-year wedding!'

'Okay, Muriel, good. Is there a timeframe?'

'Hey, I'm no Muriel. I'm not constantly fantasising about getting married.' (I had of course fantasised, but not constantly, and I hadn't been trying on dresses – there was a difference. And I was reminded to re-watch the old Aussie classic *Muriel's Wedding*.)

Peta coughed and laughed. 'Bullshit.'

'Can we focus, please? Is there a timeframe, Alice?' Liza asked again.

'By my thirtieth birthday!' Had she been hearing me at all? But Liza was just in lawyer mode, double-checking the facts.

'Right, that gives us just under two years. Now, how would you define Mr Right, Alice?' Liza was talking to me as though I was a client and she was questioning me on the stand. I didn't mind, though, because it was all helpful.

'You want a definition?'

'Well, in order to know who Mr Right is when you meet him, you should have some idea of what you're looking for.' Liza was so, so organised. 'You talk and I'll scribe. Let's start with the most obvious of your requirements. What *must* he be or have?'

'He must be single, straight and wanting to be in a relationship. Not like Gus, who was already in a relationship, or bi-Max, who was just discovering his sexuality at the age of twenty-five, or Richard, who preferred watching football to having sex.' At least my past lovers had taught me something.

'Did Richard really choose the game over you?' Peta was astonished. She'd known him from around the traps as well.

'Sure thing. I asked him straight out if he'd rather go to the football or spend the afternoon making love, and his response was . . .'

The girls waited anxiously for the answer.

'Depends on which code!'

'What!' they all screamed. I was sure my neighbours could hear us.

'Okay, so what else? Let's keep it moving, Alice.' Liza sat with pen poised.

'He must be good to his mother and like children – because clearly they're all going to be around at some point.'

'And because there's a good chance that you won't like his mum *or* the kids.' Dannie was on a comedy roll.

I kept adding to the list. 'I want him to love his job. Scott used to complain all the time about his work, I couldn't stand it. He acted like he had no control over his own happiness there. He was such a bloody victim.'

Liza was writing furiously.

'I want a man who is only addicted to me.'

'Your problem, Alice, is that it's always just about you,' Dannie said. She turned and looked directly at me. 'No addictions? None at all? Who are you going to date, a bloody priest? Can he drink coffee?'

'Coffee, yes; beer for breakfast like JC, not on your life. One alcoholic in my life is one too many. Now fill me up!' I held out my glass for another drink. Peta did the honours and we all laughed.

'I want him to think I'm the most gorgeous woman on the planet.' The others nodded in agreement: it was a fair request for any girl to make.

'And I don't want him to adore me because I'm Black. I don't want to be someone's "exotic other". Do you know how David used to introduce me?'

'How?' they asked in chorus.

'This is Alice, she's Wiradyuri.'

'What?'

'I know, I know, and he'd say it to whitefellas, like I was some freak. He didn't understand it was different when *I* said it, to place myself. That he didn't need to do it at dinner parties.'

'So what did you do?'

'I'd say "This is David, he's my own personal anthropologist."' We laughed some more.

'Anything else for the list, Alice?' Liza was the only one truly keeping on track.

'He *has* to be non-racist, non-fascist and non-homophobic, and believe in something, preferably himself. And, apropos of nothing, he must be punctual.'

'But you can be on Koori time whenever you want, right?' Dannie couldn't help herself.

'Correct,' Peta chipped in.

'He must be romantic and be comfortable with showing affection in public, and by that I don't mean grabbing me on the tit every time he kisses me.'

'Who did that?' Peta wanted to know.

'Jason, the young surfer I met down the coast last New Year's. Every time we kissed he grabbed my left breast, didn't matter where we were.'

'Why not your right one?' Peta asked.

'Left one's slightly bigger. He loved it more,' I said matter-of-factly. The discussion was getting off track again, so I brought it back. 'I want a man who is financially secure and hopefully debt-free.'

'What about a mortgage?' Liza asked.

'A mortgage is fine. I just don't want him working twenty-four/seven to pay off his gambling debts.'

'*Now* who are you outing?' Dannie said. 'You're a bloody serial dater, Alice.'

'Grant – remember him? We met at the Leukemia Foundation ball. Turned out he backed the horses to the point where he was working seventy hours a week to cover his debts. That's not the kind of man I want to marry. Would anyone?'

'Depends, was he built?' Peta always managed to bring it back to basics.

'Okay, you've got a pretty strong list here, Alice. Anything else you want to add?' Liza was trying to wrap up her side of the work. She'd been a very objective scribe and facilitator.

'Yes, I want a loyal, faithful, sincere, chivalrous, witty, competent and responsible man.' I was completely serious, but Dannie burst into giggles.

'That's it, then?' Liza asked, almost impatiently.

'No. Can you add that he should be a good communicator as well?'

'You've got to be kidding, Alice. I've never met *any* man like the one you're looking for,' Dannie said, marvelling at the long list of criteria I'd come up with.

'What about George?'

Dannie squealed with laughter. 'George! That's it, I'm going to pee myself! You live in a fantasy world sometimes, Alice.' She got up off the sofa and ran along the hall to the bathroom.

'Well, Alice, no-one could accuse you of not aiming high.' Even Liza, whose standards were generally rather exacting, was surprised at what I expected in a potential partner.

'Based on previous experience, as you have just heard, sis, I've got to aim high. The more you ask for, the more you're likely to get, right?'